The Je

[illegible]

by Kathleen L. Moore

Cover Art by the author.

The Jewelled Kingdom

The Jewelled Kingdom- Book 1, Volume 1

Kathleen L. Moore

Published by Kathleen L. moore, 2022.

THE JEWELLED KINGDOM

First edition. November 29, 2022.

ISBN: 979-8215858028

Written by Kathleen L. Moore.

Table of Contents

To my children, grandchildren and all the other children that I've met along the way.

‘The Jewelled Kingdom’

(Need Will Find the Way)

Chapter One- The Book

Looking at the clock, Rose realized that she didn't have much time before she had to pick up Amey at the train station. She'd been distracted since the letter from Robert Stall, her publisher, came saying a book reviewer wanted to interview her and wanted to contact her directly. Even though he grumbled about an author needing to promote herself, she told Robert to have him write to her in care of the publishing house. He thought all this 'mystery person' routine was a bit much but she remained adamant.

She needed something calming before she went to pick up Amey and went to make tea. Writing the book had been more an exercise in catharsis than anything else. She wasn't sure why she had sent it to the publisher in the first place. She had planned to use the story in the book to finally tell Amey the truth about their past just as her mother had always wanted. This vacation time would get it all out into the open.

Rose took her tea to the window seat overlooking the sun-filled field. She was slight of build like her daughter but not as tall. She had fair hair and complexion and her eyes a clear aquamarine that were strained with concern for her daughter. She sat on the window seat leaning back against the frame trying to calm her mind. Amey had to be told because she held the answer. Neither Rose's personal powers nor her mother's were anywhere near what Amey had been born with.

After all the years, Rose still grieved the loss of her husband just as their life together was beginning. It was a constant ache in her heart and made her all that more fearful of losing her daughter to the same evil that took her husband away from her. The Magician had taken everything from them- husband, home, kingdom and a daughter's father gone to a power-hungry maniac.

Her mother Angeline had seen Amey's aptitude for the stones first and had made it her duty to train the girl how to use the power that she didn't yet fully understand. They would go up into the mountain together to search for the gemstones that were the center of their power. Her mother taught Amey the properties of each stone and their use. She had learned the lessons well. At seventeen, she could use the stones to calm, knew how to cleanse and charge them and could even heal minor problems if the need arose. She hadn't been tested yet but the power was there in waiting – the given power of the earth that was focused through the gemstones. The extent of Amey's powers had yet to be tapped.

Rose's mind wasn't calmed by the tea. She had the first feeling of true unease even as the door to the yard burst open and Jasper rushed in saying,

"Rose, there are some men coming up the drive. I have a bad feeling about them and I think you need to get away. I don't like this coming on the heels of that letter from your publisher. "

"Jasper, what about Amey. I can't just run off and leave her behind! If I'm not there to pick her up, she will just take a cab and come home. She can't be placed in danger."

"Yes, you can and you will go. Leave her to me. I will see her safe. I want you to go to the glade. You will be met there. I have sent a message on ahead. Take what you need quickly and go."

Rose stood uncertain for a moment looking at Jasper then went to the cabinet and removed an embroidered blue velvet bag, a leather-bound book and a small box that she placed in the pockets of her jacket as she was putting it on.

"Take good care of her Jasper. She is everything."

The two burly men shifted uneasily under the unrelenting stare of the man they stood before. He was relaxed in his deck chair watching them.

Their nerves were stretched to breaking point when he finally spoke. The magician, Balik, was an intimidating man.

'You have failed me once. Do not fail me again. Bring me the queen and her daughter alive and find the stone.'

The two men didn't move to leave. They hadn't been dismissed. They watched nervously as their employer got up and walked around the deck. He stood looking out across the water to the dock. He watched the people standing in the sun.

'Do not underestimate them. Bring them both here but wait until it is dark so that they cannot attract attention.'

One of the men found the courage to speak.

'Sir? What if there is no one home?'

Balik seated himself again before he spoke.

'I want those women. You will wait until they return unless you find the stone first. Bring that to me immediately.'

He reached for the wine glass on the table. He looked up at them and the silence drew their gaze.

'Do not fail me. I will not be forgiving. Now go.'

The men turned and quickly left the deck. They breathed a sigh of relief and headed down the gangplank to the waiting black limousine. They were determined to be successful this time.

Chapter Two – Home

The slowing speed of the train alerted the young woman seated midway down the coach. She marked her place in her book and set it down on the seat. The conductor walking down the aisle announced,

'Ten minutes to Grenian station.' When she raised her head, he smiled at the slim girl with raven black hair and amazing lavender eyes. She smiled also and turned toward the window to get a better view. Leaning on the window ledge, she took in the sun-drenched scene. Amethyst Fairfield never tired of the beauty of the valley that she called home.

The train entered the Grenian Valley on the south side almost at the midpoint. A stream ran gaily from the train corridor and joined up with the Grenian River that had started its journey to the sea up in the glaciers of the Coast range to the east. Looking out over the craggy mountain peaks formed by ancient volcanic action, Amey was excited at the prospect of her trip to search for gemstones over the next three weeks. The forces that formed the Valley had also created a wide variety of gem and semi-precious stones that her family prized. She often went into the mountains with her grandmother searching for them.

Across from her, the sunlight bathed the lovely white farmhouse in its glow. It was clearly visible as the trees had yet to leaf out fully. The house had dark green trim accenting the windows and a wrap-around verandah. It was nestled back among the trees at the foot of the mountain that rose dramatically towering over it. This was Bear Claw Mountain or that's what she called it, as it resembled a gigantic black bear claw scraping the sky and that was Faerfield Farm - her home.

The train followed the southern edge of the mountains beside the river west to the coastal town of Grenian and the railway station down by the wharves. Amey leaned back in her seat and watched the landscape pass by. As the train rounded a curve, Amey could see the town in the distance with the harbour beyond.

She picked up her backpack, opened the side pocket and pushed her geology book in next to the green velvet bag. Making sure to refasten the binding securely, Amey placed the backpack on the seat beside her in order to be ready when the train came to a stop.

The docks were on the south side of the tracks and Amey turned to look at the harbour that sparkled in the noonday sun with a variety of boats bobbing in the gentle swell.

The train pulled in to the station stopping in front of the open doors leading to the waiting room and small café off to the right. Amey picked up her backpack, swung it over her shoulders and moved into the aisle to head to the exit. Stepping down onto the platform, she moved aside to let the rest of the passengers disembark. When the crowd thinned, she walked to the waiting room. Not here. A quick look at the clock confirmed that they were on time. Her mother wasn't. Taking a coin from her pocket, Amey went to the phone and called home. The phone rang but no one answered. Her mother was probably on her way.

At the information desk, she told the woman behind the counter who she was and where she was going in case her mother came. She walked out to the platform to take advantage of the wonderful, sunny day. The sun was high above and the gentle breeze from the water ruffled her hair bringing the scent of the saltwater. Some of the fishing fleet were already tied up and there was one beautifully elegant white yacht docked on the private quay. A white jacketed crewman served a table on the canopied aft deck. A sleek black car idled alongside of the yacht and two men dressed alike walked down the gangplank and got in the back. The black car turned and sped off toward the River Road exit.

Amey loved the view of the inlet with its soaring wooded slopes, circling seabirds and the sparkling, sun-kissed water. Sitting on a rock at the edge of the yard, she basked in the warmth of the sun and watched the activity down on the wharf. After a while, Amey checked her watch and decided not to wait any longer. She would take a cab to the farm. They could watch for her mother and stop her if they met. There was a Grenian Valley cab stand just outside of the station with a cabbie reading his newspaper. Amey went up and asked,

"Are you available to take me out to Faerfield Farm?"

The cabbie put down his paper and said,

"Sure. Climb in. Do you have any bags you need me to get for you?"

"No. I just have my backpack." Amey climbed in the back seat and said to the driver, "My mother was supposed to pick me up but she must have been delayed. Can we watch for her truck as we drive?"

"Sure. If you see her vehicle coming, just tell me and I'll flash my lights at her."

They left the parking lot and turned onto the River Road that ran all the way up the valley, past Faerfield Farm and further to the mountain pass leading out of the valley.

"Home for spring break, are you miss," said the driver?

"Yes," Amey replied. "What a beautiful day!"

"It's been like this all week," replied the driver. "It looks like you'll have some nice weather for your time home. Where do you go to school?"

"I attend a private school in Alerton. I have just over three weeks this year. The teachers have a training course and they gave us an extra week. If the weather holds, I'll be able to go hiking in the mountains."

Amey always looked forward to their forays into the mountain as they searched for the gemstones found there. They would also take field trips out of the Valley & up to the plateau for specimens not found at home. Grandmother would bring back more exotic gems from her numerous trips to far-off places so they had a considerable and varied collection. While mother would join them from time to time, she preferred to stay on the farm most of the time.

They did not see her mother on their way. Amey was glad she had decided to take a cab, as she would have still been waiting. Now she would be home before her mother remembered that she was supposed to pick her up. She couldn't wait to razz her on her forgetfulness.

They were approaching the gates to the farm.

"You can let me out at the gate, sir. I'll walk in from there."

Amey paid the fare and the cabbie drove off with a friendly wave. She hoisted her pack and stood there in the sun with her head thrown back breathing in the aroma of the cedars and the sun-warmed earth. This was the scent of home and, with a happy laugh, she turned and put her hand on the gate. She was surprised when it opened to her touch. They always kept the gate latched. She pushed it open, walked through then latched it behind her.

She stopped. She realized that there wasn't a sound. That was unusual as you could always hear the birds in the trees. Amey felt a tingle of apprehension as she slowed her steps to figure out what had alarmed her. She cocked her head to the side listening. There wasn't any sound at all and there should have been. She stepped to the west side of the road closer to the trees that would offer her protection while looking in all directions to see what she felt in her bones was a threat. On the point of turning to look behind her, a hand came over her mouth shutting off the scream that tried to escape. She struggled to free herself only to be pulled in tighter against the man behind her. He leaned his head to her ear and whispered in a familiar voice,

'Quiet, Amey. Look'

Earlier.

Jasper headed from the house to the group of gigantic cedars that bordered the patio. He smiled a small smile. Amey thought that she was the only one who knew the secret of the cedars but Jasper had been aware of their special feature long before she was born. The trees had grown up so close together they appeared one. Their trunks meshed and overlapped to a height of six feet before becoming separate trees again. When he reached the trees, he turned sideways and slid between one of the folds that wasn't visible unless you knew exactly where to look. He watched for the approach of the men from this hiding place. Hopefully, he could find out what their intentions were. He sensed the evil of them and felt that they must have come from the Magician. They carefully approached the back door.

"I don't see anyone inside," whispered the first man to get to the window. "It's awfully quiet. Do you think we missed them?"

"No, the truck is still here. Let's go in and find what we were sent to find before they come back."

"They haven't locked up or anything, so, they're not far. You look through those cabinets and I will go upstairs to search the rooms."

With that, he turned and went through the archway that led to the stairs. The first man went to the cabinets carefully opening drawers and rifling through everything in them. He opened cabinet doors to search among the shelves. Not finding what he was looking for, he headed to the cupboards in the kitchen and went through all the drawers and shelves coming away empty-handed. He looked around for any other places to search.

Upstairs, the second man went into the room that had a sweater draped over the back of a chair. He opened dresser drawers as carefully as the first man downstairs. He systematically searched through everything in them. When he was finished, he turned to the closet and searched the shelves- even the pockets of the clothes hanging there. Nothing.

Across the hall, there were two rooms– one smaller than the other. He stepped across to one of the rooms and decided he might as well search both. When he opened a drawer in the dresser in the smaller room, he found a box that contained rough stones of all colours. It didn't look like what was described to him but he put it in his bag anyway. He was satisfied that he wouldn't find anything else.

The man downstairs stopped when his partner came down.

"Find anything yet?"

"Not a thing. What about you?"

"Maybe. I found a box with some stones in it. They don't look like what was described but we'll take them back to the boat to see if they are what he wants. We'll come back later and bring the women to the boat.

Before the men left, Jasper crept out of his hiding place to circle around the long way back to the driveway in order to intercept Amey. He wasn't sure that he would be able to take on two men he assumed were armed.

Chapter Three- Escape

Rose ran through the woods careful to make as little sound as possible. She wished that she could go back and get Amey but knew that Jasper didn't need to worry about her safety also. Rose just had to trust him and get to the grove away from danger herself. The trees overhead gave her a semblance of security from prying eyes. She followed a faint path among the trees used on their trips to the mountain. As she came closer to the stream, the trees began to change from cedars and other evergreens to include more birch, alder and the willow which loved to be near the water.

Jasper's reaction made her fear that the men were sent by the Magician. She had to assume that he had means to enter this world and her book on 'The Jewelled Kingdom' had led him to her. She was sure he had no idea that Amey was Alair's daughter. Rose hadn't known that she was pregnant when she escaped and only discovered her pregnancy after they moved to the farm. That secret would protect Amey.

Rose rested her hand on a mossy, twisted trunk and reached into her pocket for the velvet bag. It was beautifully detailed with golden threads in a pattern of shapes and ancient symbols. She put her hand into the bag and withdrew without looking a clear crystal of purest quartz. Rose walked to the path leading to the glade. She cleared her mind of all thought but what she needed now. The glade had a sacred quality that soothed the soul. Rose held the crystal in her hand to the center of her breast, breathed in deeply and, when she was at peace, prayed the ancient words of the ritual. She chanted softly and felt the power of the crystal flow through her. She held the energy in check and wasn't afraid when she heard a gentle voice "You are safe, milady," he said. "Come, we must go now."

And where Rose stood but moments before there was now only the faintest residual shimmer.

Jasper had been right. A taxi drew up outside the gate. Amey paid the driver and got out. She stood there with a smile on her face enjoying the sun. A puzzled look crossed her face as the gate opened under her hand but she continued in and latched it securely behind her. She started to walk up the drive clearly enjoying herself but suddenly stopped and cocked her head at the silence.

"Good girl," Jasper thought. "You sense something is wrong. You have good instincts."

He watched as she moved over to the side of the road where the larger evergreens grew and toward where he was concealed. He quietly moved to where she would enter. Just as she reached a larger tree, Amey sensed him behind her and started to turn. He put his hand over her mouth to cut off the startled scream he could feel rising in her throat and held her tightly. He leaned his head to her ear and whispered,

"Quiet, Amey. Look."

She stilled and watched the car driving from the house. When they reached the gate, one got out of the car to open it for the chauffeur to drive through. Aware that Amey had latched the gate, he was ready to pull her to safety if the chauffeur alerted the man. Obviously, the driver thought little of it as he drove through the open gate and stopped just on the other side waiting for him to close it again and climb back in the car. The car turned toward town and sped off.

Jasper removed his hand from Amey's mouth and turned her to him. She was wide eyed but didn't appear to be afraid.

"Jasper! What is this all about? I saw that car down on the private dock by a huge white yacht. Something felt wrong here just before you put your hand over my mouth. There were no birds singing. What's going on? Where are my mother and Grandmother?"

"They are safe, Amey. I sent your mother away before those men got to the house"

Jasper took her hand and led her deeper into the woods.

"We will be going after her. Before that, though, I need to tell you something. We have to slip into the house and collect some supplies. Hurry, though. We need to get away from here."

Amey followed behind Jasper with a thousand thoughts running through her head. She was confused and beginning to worry. Where were her mother and Grandmother? Why had Jasper sent her mother away? Who were those men and why was Jasper in such a hurry? She wondered what it was that he needed to tell her but knew that she would have to wait. Looking up, she realized that the birds were singing again.

Chapter Four – The Meeting

The wind was driving the rain hard into the face of the cloaked woman who struggled to keep her feet under her.

'No one who saw me now would believe me to be a queen," thought Angeline. "Good thing too."

Indeed, there was no place for her to be a queen. All had been destroyed long ago and now Altidio and Freo were as one country.

She pulled the edges of the cloak back together as the wind sought to pull it out of her hand. It was only a short distance to go and she knew that a warm fire awaited her. The storm had come up so quickly that she had been completely taken by surprise. A little earlier, Angeline had sent the boy Galen on ahead to make sure everything was ready. He attracted no undue attention being only one of many boys seen around in the streets looking for small jobs. She had no idea how many would be coming especially with the beastly weather. She had been encouraged by the steadfast support that she'd received at the other gatherings she'd assembled to raise up her people to stand against the Magician.

Her cloak was soaked and heavy on her shoulders and she was greatly relieved to see the warehouse not too far distant. It wasn't safe to meet in people's homes and expose them to danger so Angeline had young Galen scout out empty buildings that wouldn't attract too much attention if a number of people were to gather there. Smoke rose from the chimney at the back of the sturdy, unpainted building whose fading sign read 'Bergun's Warehouse.' Even faced with the thought of a warm fire, Angeline cautiously approached the side of the building where she could peek through the window to be sure all was safe. The room beyond was cluttered with barrels and boxes but there would be enough room for them. Galen was sitting on the floor in front of the cast iron stove warming his hands. His dark curls were in disarray from the wind and rain. He'd opened his small pack and munched on the sandwich that Angeline had given him. Considering it safe, she tapped on the window. His head swung around and he jumped up and quickly opened the door.

"Come in, milady," he said. "I have the fire going really good. Let me take your cloak and hang it up to dry."

Angeline gladly took off the sopping garment and Galen hung it from a nail near the stove. Her shirt and long pants weren't too bad and would dry quickly by the fire. Not exactly queenly garb but definitely suited to the job at hand.

"Here, milady. I found you something to sit on."

He dragged over a wooden crate and turned it on end. He placed it close to the stove and looked about trying to think what else he should do.

"Sit down, Galen, and finish your sandwich.

Galen smiled shyly and resumed his seat in front of the stove. He picked up the sandwich and continued to eat with relish. He looked up as Angeline lifted her hands to her hair dragging her fingers through the tangled mess trying to get it back in some semblance of order.

"Milady, I have a small comb, if you'd like," the boy said. He pulled one from his back pocket that had bent to the shape of his bottom. Looking at it, he became embarrassed and started to put it back in his pocket.

"Why, Galen, how amazing you are. Just what I need! Thank you so much."

Angeline reached for the comb and the boy's face lit with pleasure. It was small but did the job. Her shoulder-length hair was darkened by the rain to a dark honey colour and waved gently back from a rather lovely face. Her eyes in the gloom looked to be a dark grey but were,

in truth, an unusual shade of smoky blue. Her daughter resembled her a lot but in a brighter way.

"We shouldn't have long to wait. If anyone is going to come out it this weather they will be here soon."

Angeline got up to move around. Even in her mid-fifties she was a strong, capable looking woman of average height who exuded confidence and energy. Her eyes were alive with intelligence and her movements were quick and lithe. She was wound up tightly and hoped that she would be able to secure the support of this community in her quest. This was a large, wealthy community and the people who would come tonight would be able to bring the strongest support to the campaign against the Magician. Travelling around the kingdom enlisting the support of her people was not something she chose to leave to her loyal staff but felt it necessary to do herself. She needed their support and she wanted to show them that she cared for their welfare.

A quiet knock sounded at the door. Angeline waved Galen away and went to the door herself cracking it open to see who was there. Recognizing the leader of the group of six men and five women, Angeline opened the door to let them in. Amid greetings of "milady" she ushered the group over to the stove before she ventured to speak a word to them. They stood removing their wet hats and scarves and Galen offered to put them around to dry out a bit. Once the amenities had been seen to, Angeline calmed her mind. She needed to present the strongest case possible to sway these people.

"Thank you for coming out on such a dreadful evening. I have met all of you before at the palace on many occasions as far back as when my husband was alive. I have considered you my loyal friends and I want to assure you that I will not hold it against you if you feel, at the end of this meeting, that you cannot support me. I could do nothing else but fight to save my people from the evil of the Magician. How he turned my son-in-law against me and sought to use my daughter to bring down her own mother burns in my heart. I will use all my powers and that of those who support me to remove the Magician from his usurped position on the throne of Alair's kingdom and mine."

She paused to look into the faces of those present but couldn't read what they were thinking so she continued.

"I have received word from those who cared for my daughter while she remained in Alair's household that the Magician has turned Alair's mind to war against us. They say that he is like one in a dream and that he depends on the Magician to advise him on what he should do. We have always been a peaceful people but I believe that we have to fight to continue to be able to live that peaceful life. We are not without power. We have many resources to assist us. We mustn't allow the Magician to gain control of our kingdom. We seek to remove him from his position of power so that he is no future threat to us. I beseech you to join with me in this struggle."

Angeline fell silent and looked expectantly to the people assembled. The men and women turned to discuss among themselves and she could feel the tension build in her as she waited for their response. Galen stood beside her and Angeline reached down to grip his hand in hers. He squeezed hers back in support and, looking up to her, gave her a confident smile. She smiled in return but without the same confidence. The minutes dragged on while the men and women conferred among themselves. From time to time, one would look up at her and look away quickly. She had to move. She had turned to walk to the window when there was another quiet knock. As everyone fell silent and turned a fearful look to the door, a second quiet knock came followed by the urgent whisper,

"Milady, you need to get away. I have run here from the inn and there are a couple of wicked looking men asking questions about a woman dressed as you are. Hurry, please."

Angeline tore open the door to see a man she didn't recognize. He stepped in and continued.

"I am Carl, milady. You don't remember me but you helped my little girl when she was sick last year. I couldn't let them find you here. Please hurry."

She turned back to the men and women, saw their concern, and said,

"Hurry! You must get away! I would not cause you trouble. Thank you for coming. Go now, quickly" Galen brought them their hats and scarves and gathered up his and Angeline's things also. The last man turned as he was about to step through the door.

"Milady, we are your true friends. We will support you."

She clasped his hand and said a heartfelt

"Thank you. I'll be in touch."

She watched them melt into the darkness. Galen grabbed her hand and pulled her through the door and Carl said,

"Come this way, milady. I will see you safe."

He sped off across the street and led them a short way down the road to a small house set back in darkness. He opened the door with a key and pulled them inside the entryway.

"This is my home, milady. We can stay here in the dark and watch for the men. Perhaps you will recognize them. I saw you over at the warehouse earlier when I was going out to the inn. When I heard those men, I rushed back to warn you."

"Thank you, Carl, for your quick thinking."

There was a good view from where they were hiding. They didn't have long to wait as two burly men dressed in black raincoats and wide-brimmed hats turned into the road from the direction of the inn. They stopped a short distance from the warehouse and had a quick discussion. One of the men broke away and headed around the back of the building while the other moved more slowly to the door. He seemed to wait for something and then rushed the door, putting his shoulder to it forcing it open with a crash. He barreled into the room they had just vacated. The first man came around from the back and joined him at the door. The second man flexed his shoulders and said to him in disgust,

"There's no one here now."

"There's no back exit." said the first man.

"Someone has been here though. The room is warm and there are puddles in the dirt on the floor. A fair number from the look of the scuffles in the dust. Women too. We're too late. The boss isn't going to be pleased."

"It's not our fault, is it? He can't blame us! They weren't here."

The first man looked over to him with a sneer on his face. He saw the fear in his eyes and, though he wouldn't admit it himself, felt some of the same fear in his belly.

"Since when has that made any difference to him? Let's get back and get this over with. The stones weren't the ones he wanted and we didn't bring him either the daughter or the mother. The Magician isn't going to be too pleased about that at all. Come on."

Together they turned and walked back the way they had come. They weren't moving as confidently now. When they reached the corner, they disappeared from sight.

Angeline gripped the doorframe when her legs became suddenly weak. Her heart was in her throat with the fear that those words instilled. Her daughter? Those ruthless men had been to the farm! The Magician had found them! She had to get control of herself so that she could think. Surely Jasper had gotten her away otherwise they would've had Rose. What about Amey? She had to contact Jasper.

"Carl, thank you so much for your timely help. Can I ask you for a place where I can sit quietly for a while?"

"Of course, milady. Come; let me light a lamp and you can use any part of my home you wish. The wife is away visiting her sister. So's my daughter. This young fella and I will just go for a walk and give you some peace."

Carl knew the powers that the queen possessed from her treatment of his daughter when she was so sick last fall. He was in awe of what he had seen and would've done anything she asked out of gratitude for the life of his child.

"Come on, young man. We'll go find some food for milady and bring it back."

"Is that what you want, milady?"

Galen was unsure whether he should leave her alone and Angeline saw the concern in his eyes.

"It's alright, Galen. Go with Carl and let me be for a bit. I need to do something right away. You and Carl go and get some food for us. We will have to leave quickly when you come back."

With that, she placed her hand on his head ruffling his curls and smiled in reassurance. Galen smiled in return and said as he was leaving,

"We won't be too long, milady. We'll keep our ears open for any news also."

Angeline closed the door behind them and took the lamp Carl had lit for her. She walked from the entry into the small living room. It was shabby but scrupulously clean. She placed the lamp on a small table by the handmade rocking chair. She chose to sit in the middle of the colourful braided rug, crossed her legs under her and breathed deeply releasing the tension in her shoulders. She reached under her shirt and removed a small purple velvet bag embroidered with symbols in silver thread. She undid the clasp and removed a clear quartz crystal. Holding the crystal in both hands, she raised her closed hands to her forehead letting the energy of the stone enter her being. She controlled her breathing, clearing everything else from her mind concentrating on the breathing alone. The power of the crystal filled her mind, expanding her consciousness. She invoked the ancient prayer and spoke the words of the ritual. Her consciousness expanded to fill the room.

She waited. The humming was soothing and she breathed easily to its rhythm. Time didn't exist. Still, she waited.

"Jasper, where are you? Where is Rose?"

"I am at the farm. I sent Rose to Lirin. She waits for you at the lodge. We are safe."

Relief flooded her body.

"Thank God! Jasper, the men were here who say they came to the farm. What about Amey?"

"I waited for Amey to arrive. We will come there soon also."

"Thank you, Jasper. Galen and I will leave for the lodge as soon as we can."

The awareness faded and Angeline sat quietly with her eyes closed letting peace fill her being. She stretched her shoulders and rested her hands in her lap as she offered up a prayer of thanks. Refreshed and relieved she opened her eyes and put the crystal back in the bag closing it securely. She rose and walked around the small house noting the poverty but also their pride in the small dwelling. She smiled. This was their palace. Angeline reached into her pants pocket and removed another velvet bag. Inside this bag were a variety of stones. She chose a lovely green tourmaline stone. This stone would provide protection for this small family's spiritual and physical being.

Angeline heard the boy Galen and Carl return. They entered the livingroom carrying a small bag. Galen rushed in saying,

"We couldn't get much but there are some apples and bread. We also have a bottle of grape juice and a couple pieces of cheese."

He was such a sweet boy. Angeline turned to Carl and, taking his hands in hers, said,

"Thank you again. Open your hand. This stone is a tourmaline. I give it to you for your family's protection. You have offered me your protection and now I offer you mine."

She closed his hand over the stone smiling at his wonder.

"You are a good man, Carl. I will remember you. Come now Galen. We must be on our way."

"Milady, it's late. Wouldn't you rather stay here for the night and get a start early in the morning?"

"No, Carl. We need to be on our way now. We will be fine. We only have a short distance to go tonight to our lodging. Thank you anyway."

Carl took up the lamp and walked them to the door.

"Galen can tell you what we heard when we were out. Goodnight, milady. God's speed."

"Good night, Carl."

They stepped out into an evening that had turned clear. The scent of the rain was in the air and moisture was a gentle caress on her face. Angeline walked down the road with Galen letting him carry the small bag.

"If you are hungry, Galen, have one of the apples. Now tell me, what did you hear?"

Galen got out one of the apples and said,

"The men came to town this afternoon. They have been everywhere asking for you. Well, not you in particular but describing you all the same. The people here didn't like the looks of them so told them they hadn't seen anyone. They were checking out buildings and must've heard of the warehouse as we did. We went by the inn and heard the people saying that the men were picked up by a carriage and left town."

"Thank you, Galen. You have done well for me today. Jasper will be proud of you. Now, let's see how fast we can get to our beds. We have an early day tomorrow."

Chapter Five– Awakening

Jasper led Amey through the dense woods around to the back of the house. They went the long way, heading toward the mountain and coming out at the twisted cedars near the patio. When Amey started to go ahead, he held her back and stood quietly listening. Amey strained to hear any unusual sounds. The sun was warm through the trees and the cedars gave off their pungent spicy fragrance. Where before there had been deadly silence, you could now hear the birds singing in the trees and the many common nature sounds of the countryside. Still, he stood a while longer until he was satisfied that it was safe for them to head for the house.

"We are not staying long, Amey," he said with his hand on her shoulder. "I want you to collect all the things you will need for an extended trip- things that you would've packed to go on hiking trips with your grandmother. Take important things but keep your load to a minimum because we will be moving quickly."

When Amey started to speak, he cut her off saying,

"I will explain all this as best I can when we are somewhere safe. Trust me, Amey. Go gather your things and I will collect some supplies for us."

With a small shove toward the hallway, he turned into the kitchen and left Amey standing bewildered. She didn't hesitate long though but went up to her room.

When she was gone, Jasper opened his mind to the sensation he felt and reached for Angeline. He wanted to assure her that he had Amey safe and that he was bringing her to Altidio.

"Jasper, where are you? Where is Rose?"

"I am at the farm. I sent Rose to Lirin. She waits for you at the lodge. We are safe."

Relief flooded her body.

"Thank God! Jasper, the men were here who say they came to the farm. What about Amey?"

"I waited for Amey to arrive. We will come there soon also."

"Thank you, Jasper. Galen and I will leave for the lodge as soon as we can."

The awareness faded and Jasper turned to fill the backpack with the supplies they would need.

Upstairs, Amey crossed to her closet and pulled out the backpack that she always used for her trips with her grandmother and set it on the chair by the dresser. Quickly gathering the essentials and carefully packing them to take as little space as possible, Amey tried to think just what was going on. She went to the top drawer of her dresser to collect the box of gemstones that she had gathered on her last trip with her grandmother only to find it missing.

"That's strange," she thought.

She looked around the room again and could now see the signs of things being out of place. Across the hall in her mother's room, she detected the same telltale signs. Their rooms had been searched! The only thing that she could see missing was her box of gemstones. They were of little value but she treasured them. Why would someone take a box of coloured stones?

Going back into her room, she quickly finished her packing. Hurrying down the stairs, she stopped at the hall closet and chose a warmer jacket to take which fit nicely into the front pocket of the backpack. On the top shelf of the closet was the small survival kit that they always took and she added it to a side pocket where she could easily reach it. She securely tied off the drawstring and closed and buckled the flap on her pack. Reaching up again she brought down the lightweight, cold weather sleeping bag and attached it to the top. Swinging the pack over her shoulders, she hitched it in place and fastened the chest and waist straps.

When she reached the kitchen, Jasper was standing at the window staring into space. He turned and bent adjusting the straps on his pack which looked considerably heavier than hers. She offered,

"Do you need me to carry anything?

"No thanks. You ready to go?"

At her nod, Jasper turned to the kitchen door and peered out the window. He opened the door a crack to listen, and, obviously finding nothing to concern him, stepped out onto the patio. He held the door for Amey and pointed toward the twisted cedars as the direction he wanted to go. Amey led off passing her secret hiding place to the woods beyond.

They set off on roughly the same path that Rose had taken earlier but Jasper didn't plan on going to the glade. He was heading for the cave a ways up the mountain. He needed to sit down in a place he could be sure of with Amey and tell her some of what was happening. She needed to know why they were running and where they were going. Her mother had been putting off telling her of her history and it put Jasper in the unenviable position of telling Amey a story she might have difficulty believing. She needed to be prepared for an unusual experience and get some idea of what part she could be playing in it all.

"Head off toward the rock fall, Amey. You know of the cave up there?"

"Yes. Grandmother and I used to go there to get out of the rain sometimes."

"That's where we're going. I need to tell you what's happening. We'll stay there tonight and get an early start tomorrow. OK?"

She nodded and Jasper took the lead now. He was grateful that Amey was being patient and not asking all the questions he knew she had a right to ask.

Jasper struck off to the northwest. The forest floor was littered with the remains of fallen giants that wore green blankets of moss. Young seedlings sprouted on the tops of mouldering logs and they stepped around trunks as high as their shoulders. There was no discernable path but the two of them had been in these woods since Amey was small and knew where they were going. They walked in silence. Occasional shafts of light speared through a break in the canopy but, the closer they traveled to the mountain, the less they would see the sun. The cave where they were headed faced west and would catch the dying rays. The sun would have warmed the stone and they would be comfortable there.

More rock began to show on the forest floor and the ground began to rise slightly. The footing became more treacherous and they had to watch where they put their feet. Soon bigger rock began appearing and they had to pick their way through the rubble. The trees here weren't the giants from before but smaller trees that grew up in between the slides that cleared large swaths of trees out of its path from time to time. They were on the edge of the slide zone and the climb led up through the jumble of stone that had collected over time. They would have no breath for talking and would need to concentrate on their foot placement. Some of the rocks weren't safe to step on. Even though her pack wasn't heavy when she put it on, Amey felt the weight as she climbed. She knew that Jasper's load was much heavier than hers but he moved with agility over the rocks and boulders. She wasn't used to this amount of exertion. She would normally have worked up to a hike of this nature over a few days after getting home from school. Certainly not directly off the train but she wouldn't complain.

Jasper realized that this was quite a hike for someone who hadn't been hiking for a while. He stopped in a small open area and set his pack on the rocks. He pulled open the side pocket and took out an apple and removed a small container of water from where it hung on the outside. He looked up as Amey came into the clearing wiping the sweat from her face.

"Here," he said and passed her the water bottle and the apple. Amey sank gratefully to one of the rocks, loosed her pack and let it slide down to rest on the ground. She took the bottle and drank gratefully. She passed it back to Jasper.

"Thanks," she said breathlessly. "I'm out of shape!"

Jasper just smiled and took a drink before hanging the bottle back on his pack. He took a second bottle from his pack and hooked it to a grommet on Amey's. He sat down on a rock and leaned back on one that rose behind it.

She took a bite of the apple and sighed as the sweet juice ran down her throat. She realized that she hadn't eaten since breakfast and wished she'd bought something in the café. When she had finished the apple, Amey eased her shoulders and stretched her arms over her head, arching her back to take out the stiffness. The cooler air after the exertion felt good on her face. She should've thought to change into more rugged clothes although the grey slacks and purple long sleeved light wool t-shirt she wore were durable. She looked over at Jasper who was watching an eagle wheel in the thermals above the mountain. He caught her glance and turned to her and asked,

"Ready to go again or do you want more time?"

Being young and fit, Amey had recovered her wind so she said,

"Let's go" and got up pulling her pack to her shoulders again. Jasper hoisted his as well and they continued their climb.

The way was challenging but not really too hard. They didn't go too quickly but at a pace that Jasper matched to Amey's. The cave wasn't much farther up the slope. It wasn't a large cave but had a good overhang and sides that jutted out creating a windbreak. Jasper started to pick up small pieces of wood to replenish what was always kept there. Amey saw what he was doing and also picked up what pieces she could find. The break had given her just the rest that she needed and she felt refreshed.

They reached the cave while the sun was still shining in the opening. They both removed their packs and sat down to enjoy the warm rays. They sat that way for a short time but, when the sun's rays began to leave their resting place, they got up and pulled out their jackets knowing that the temperature would fall quickly this high up in the mountain. The day was ending swiftly with the sun's departure. Jasper moved to the woodpile at the back of the cave and built a small fire in the ring of rocks on the floor. The dry twigs caught quickly and he fed in larger pieces until he had a cheery blaze going. The cave had breaks in the wall that allowed the smoke to dissipate without looking like the mountain was on fire and attracting attention to the spot. Jasper had looked before from the farm when he knew someone was in the cave and was satisfied that no one would notice the smoke.

Amey took her sleeping bag from her pack and laid it out on one side of the fire as she saw Jasper doing on the other. She sat on her bag and looked into the flames. After a while Jasper broke the silence saying,

"It's time I explained what's happening. But before I do that, I need to tell you a story. I don't want you to say anything until I'm finished." He began,

"About seventeen years ago, a woman married a wonderful young man. He was handsome and lived in a country that bordered hers. His parents were very pleased with the match and they and her mother saw them away on their honeymoon. While they were away, his parents were killed by someone who wanted their wealth and power. He tried to kill her mother also but she escaped unhurt.

The couple came back immediately and the husband was heartbroken as he deeply loved his parents. He was inconsolable. He had an older distant cousin who came for the funeral and moved in to the family home. Soon it became clear that the cousin didn't have the young man's best interest at heart and he somehow gained control over the grief-stricken young man's mind. He suggested that his mother-in-law wanted to take advantage of him and tried to influence the young woman against her own mother also.

But the young woman realized what he was doing and tried to tell her husband that his cousin was evil and only wanted to take what rightfully belonged to him, her husband. But the evil cousin had an answer for that also and caused doubt to enter the young man's mind concerning the wife he loved. Friends of the wife who lived close by didn't know what to do for the couple and helped the wife get away from her husband when he wouldn't be swayed by her reasoning. She returned to her mother and found out she also escaped from death in a similar accident that took her in-laws lives. The evil cousin then sent people to harm both the mother and daughter and destroy their home. They gathered their precious things and ran away. They went to another country, changed their names and hid. The evil cousin couldn't find them and they gradually felt safe."

Jasper paused.

"That's the story of 'The Jewelled Kingdom," said Amey. "I have been reading Mother's book again. I find it so sad."

Jasper continued,

"What the book doesn't say is that the young wife found out not long after that she was going to have a baby. She felt grateful that the evil cousin hadn't known of this but sad about her husband not knowing about his child. She knew, however, that she couldn't let him know when he was under the influence of the cousin. So, mother and daughter lived together and, in time, a lovely little girl was born. The young mother was overjoyed as her beautiful daughter looked just like her father but grieved for the husband she'd lost."

"Yes," said Jasper, "the story is sad but it is also the story of your family. Your Grandmother is the Queen of 'the Jewelled Kingdom' and your mother the young wife who married Prince Alair and you are the lovely baby girl who was born in exile."

Amey leaped to her feet.

'What?' Amey was dazed. 'Why didn't they tell me? I had a right to know!'

She couldn't take it in. Why? She felt betrayed. Surely, she had a right to know about her history and that she had a father who was alive. Wasn't this information important for her to know? At the moment, she couldn't even remember what she had been told so long ago about her father. She hadn't understood why her mother had written under another name and been so adamant about no one knowing who she really was. She thought she knew why now. She had been afraid of discovery. But why had she written the book at all? Why not just tell the story to her! She now asked that of Jasper.

"Why did she write the book if she was afraid of being found?"

"She was writing the book to be able to explain to you about your history. She couldn't think of any other way to do it without it sounding like a fairy tale. She has been putting off telling you though your grandmother and I have been urging her to do it for a long time."

Amey had so many questions running through her mind.

"So, my father is still alive but he doesn't know about me. Where are these countries that we are from?"

She looked over at Jasper and he seemed to find it difficult to look back at her. He seemed uncertain.

"Amey, the story I told you was hard enough for you to take in. What I have to tell you now will be more difficult. But, please, believe that what I say to you now is true."

He wanted to tell her in a way that would be easy for her to understand although it was hard for even someone born to the knowledge to understand fully.

"Your grandmother rules the small Kingdom of Altidio and your father the neighbouring Kingdom of Freo. I can see by your face that you don't recognize these countries from any geography that you've studied. That's because they are not of this world."

When Amey would have spoken, Jasper held up his hand and said, "Please, let me finish and then I will answer your questions."

He paused again to collect his thoughts.

"Your grandmother has taught you about gemstones and their powers. You have learned how to cleanse them and charge them and do small things like cure a headache or relieve a pain. You have even been able to do simple thought sharing with your grandmother. These powers are minor compared to the true power of the stones. This power is the power of the earth- God's power through which we are able to do wondrous things. Your grandmother, mother and you all have that power. Even I also have a measure of the same power. What you need to understand is the extent of this power."

He leaned toward the fire and stared in to Amey's eyes.

"When your mother ran away from your father to her mother, they both had to escape again and used their power to leave their world and come here. They sought the power of the stones and used it to travel through dimensions. This world is on another plane from our homeland. Today, when the men came to the farm, I sent your mother back to that land to safety. Your grandmother is there now raising up her people and Prince Alair's to fight. The man they want to fight against is your father's distant cousin Balik, a powerfully evil magician. The people are banding together to fight against him. He is here now in this world and sent those men to the farm today. He needs to kill your family because their power is a threat to him. He doesn't know about you and that is good. Why is your grandmother only now banding the people together to fight? Because of you. From when you were young, your grandmother recognized that yours is an extraordinary power- a power that could defeat the magician when joined with theirs and all the others who have power."

Amey was stunned. She had no power. She was just a girl.

"How is this possible? It goes against all rational thought!"

"Anything is possible with God's power, Amey. That there are other dimensions to our universe is not a new concept. I do not fully understand it I only know that it is."

Jasper looked at Amey tenderly. This was a lot for her to take in. He wished that there was some way to make it easier for her. Perhaps there was a way to prove it to her.

"Amey, were going to try an experiment. Take out your crystal."

Amey reached into her pack and pulled out the green velvet bag. She opened the clasp, pulled open the drawstring, and slipped her hand in removing her crystal. It was about the size of a walnut, elongated and many-faceted.

"Now I want you to clear you mind as your grandmother taught you and relax. Breathe deeply and concentrate on your breath." He waited until he saw her begin to relax. "Now, cup your hands around the crystal and bring your cupped hands up to your forehead. Breathe deeply and let the power of the stone enter your being."

He paused and watched her to see if she was able to achieve the state she needed. What he saw comforted him.

"Think of your grandmother. Picture her. I want you to repeat after me."

He paused again to give her time.

"By Your power I am empowered. Open the way for me."

Amey repeated,

"By Your power I am empowered. Open the way for me."

"Again!"

"By Your power I am empowered. Open the way for me."

"Now call to your grandmother. Ask her to hear you."

"Grandmother, hear me."

Amey's voice was tentative.

"Again, but with more confidence."

Amey repeated with a stronger voice.

"Grandmother, hear me!"

An unusual feeling filled Amey's body. She felt something ...more. Her mind felt full. She was puzzling over this sensation when she heard her grandmother's voice.

"I am here, Amey. "

Amey was startled and the feeling started to fade. Jasper urged her to concentrate and the feeling returned more strongly.

"Grandmother?"

"Yes, Amey, I am here. Jasper has told you?"

It wasn't so much a question as a worried plea.

"Yes, Grandmother. I don't understand!"

"It will be alright, Amey. Jasper is bringing you here. Your mother and I will be waiting. Get some sleep and don't worry."

Amey suddenly felt tired. The fullness left her and she found herself firmly back in the cave staring across the fire at Jasper. Her eyes were wide with wonder. She couldn't say anything. He smiled gently at her.

"That was well done, Amey. Your grandmother is right. Get some sleep. We will talk again in the morning."

"You could hear her too?"

"Yes," he said. "Kind of like a conference call, eh?"

Amey burst out laughing and the tension eased from her body.

"Yes, a conference call."

She felt more tired than she expected. The excitement and novelty of the day and the revelations of the last few minutes left her drained. The anger over not being told was lessened but still there.

"I think I will turn in. Good night, Jasper."

Amey crawled into her sleeping bag and was asleep instantly.

Jasper sat looking into the fire for a little longer before he too laid down to sleep. Tomorrow would see new wonders and experiences for Amey but he knew now that she would come through just fine. Comforted, he too drifted off to sleep.

Very early the next morning, while Angeline prepared to leave their shelter, she thought back to the previous evening. Before retiring for the night, she had felt an awareness forming in her mind. A voice had called to her.

"Grandmother, hear me!"

"I am here, Amey. "

The feeling started to fade and then returned more strongly.

"Grandmother?"

"Yes, Amey, I am here. Jasper has told you?"

It wasn't so much a question as a worried plea.

"Yes, Grandmother. I don't understand!"

"It will be alright, Amey. Jasper will bring you here. Your mother and I will be waiting. Get some sleep and don't worry."

Angeline realized that they were going to find it hard to explain to Amey why she hadn't been told before. She was kicking herself that she hadn't insisted that Rose sit Amey down when she was old enough to understand and tell her of her history and that her father was still alive. Now they had to hope that she could understand and would be open to expanding her power so that they could fight the Magician.

Angeline lifted Galen down from the horse's back and tied the reins to the fence. They had left early from the safety of the shelter where they'd spent the night. Her horse had been ready and she'd thanked her hosts for their hospitality. They were one of a series of trusted supporters who eased her travelling as she sought to raise support among the people. It had taken more time than she had planned to travel here because they had to hide from the Magician's patrols. When word had come to her that her daughter, Rose, had fled the farm and was now at the Lodge, she was relieved. Jasper was now bringing Amey so they would all be together soon.

It was still early in the day and they were stopping in a small town not too far from their destination. Angeline wanted to talk to the mayor again and find out what he'd heard on the movements of the

Magician's men. They were searching the countryside and harassing anyone who might support her.

Her mind was again silent and at rest. Things were moving fast and Angeline only hoped they could adjust and somehow win the day.

Chapter Six- Homecoming

'Welcome home, milady."

The young man who grasped her hand was about twenty years of age with vivid green eyes and shoulder-length blonde hair that framed a tanned face of rugged beauty. He was taller than her and had the look of a person used to outdoor life. Strong, broad shoulders were dressed in a green woolen jacket over brown twill pants. He looked to be right at home in the woods. He was already leading her away from a glade that resembled the one she just left. Rose felt a quickening in her heart just knowing that she was home.

He led her to a spot in the woods where he had left his backpack. He noted her lack of any bag and guessed there wasn't room in her pockets for much food or drink. He reached down and lifted a water bottle from the side of his pack.

"We have a distance to travel to reach the lodge. I see you do not have any supplies with you. Are you hungry or thirsty?"

Rose realized that the excitement and fright of her headlong flight had left her still thirsty even after her drink at the stream and she gladly accepted the water that he passed to her. She drank the cool, clear water thankfully and returned his bottle saying,

"Thank you for the water but I'm not hungry at the moment. What is your name?"

"I am Lirin, Jasper's nephew. I was too young when you left for you to remember me. We received Jasper's message and I was the closest to meet with you. Come, we must go."

Rose followed behind Lirin as he headed off into the forest. The sun was high in the sky and shone through the woods in patches. Off to her right Rose could see the mass of the mountain above the trees and had that familiar start of surprise she had experienced before when she left this world so many years ago. For the mountain that she saw was the same mountain that Amey called Bear Claw. It was the landmark that drew both her and her mother so long ago when they were fleeing and it was the same landmark that had cheered their exile.

Lirin kept up a steady pace but Rose knew that he was taking it easier for her sake. His long legs could've covered much more ground were he alone. They skirted a stream that flowed from the mountain and crossed it on a gigantic fallen log that showed the usage of ages of feet. The water was running swiftly from melting snow.

Rose asked, "Lirin, is my mother at the lodge?

"Not yet but she will be there soon. She has been travelling across the two countries enlisting the support of community leaders. She might be there when we arrive or will be there soon after."

Rose's thoughts went back to the last conversation that she'd had with her mother. They had been sitting out on the patio to catch the warmth of the sun after a long winter. They had a tray with their lunch and, after eating, continued to sit out in the deck chairs drinking their tea.

"Rose, I think the time has come for me to go back again to Altidio and begin to gather the support of the community leaders. It will take quite a while to do it as it has to be done in secret."

"But Mother, don't you think we are rushing this? I haven't even told Amey about her history or that her father is still alive. We don't know how she will react! We aren't even sure about the extent of her power."

"I am sure of her power and so are you. I have felt its surge and I know the depth of her heart. Do you honestly think that she will sit back and do nothing when she hears that her father is under Balik's spell? Don't you think that she will do everything that she can to free him when she realizes that she has enough power to do so?"

Rose was torn in two. She had loved her husband passionately but that had been so long ago. But she loved her daughter fiercely and feared what this would mean.

"She's all I have left, Mother! I am afraid for her."

The plaintive note brought Angeline to her side. She hugged her close, pressing a kiss to the top of her head. She also feared for Amey and for all of them. There were no guarantees that they would win.

Angeline had secretly returned to Altidio awhile after their escape and found their home in total devastation. Barik had angrily laid waste to the palace where Angeline had lived happily with her husband the king and raised their daughter to womanhood. The people were downtrodden and little of their happy life remained. Angeline visited some of their retainers and found out as much as she could about the Magician. He had taken over the palace in Freo and no one had much news of Prince Alair. On her visits, she treated their ills as well as she could and tried to comfort them with hope for the future.

Rose had never gone back on any of Angeline's visits and, once she was pregnant, stayed close to home on the farm. She withdrew into herself and Angeline had worried about her. When the baby was born, Rose was elated but Angeline could still see the sadness in her when Rose saw that Amey resembled her father so much. She tried to reassure Rose.

"Rose. We have waited for this day a long time. We knew very early on that Amey had an unusual power and it gave us hope that one day we would be able to defeat the Magician. That we could release Alair's mind from his hold and could return to our world to live happily ever after."

She held her daughter close to her heart and rubbed comfortingly up and down her arm. She thought that she understood now what had been in her daughter's mind. She gently asked,

"Is that why you haven't told Amey – so that you could put off the day when she would be asked to use her power and join to ours and save her father and our lands?"

Rose's head jerked up to say that wasn't true but the denial died on her lips when she saw the gentle smile on her lovely mouth. She knew that her mother spoke the truth. She replied with a wry smile,

"I suppose so. I have been putting it off. For too long! It just got easier not to tell her the longer I waited. I have been writing it all down in that book and thought that when Amey read it, we could use the story as a starting place. I just couldn't think how she would react to such a wild story. Have I made a mistake? Will she resent that I kept it from her?"

" I can't say I agree with such a roundabout route but I suppose I can see how it might help. Amey is a remarkable young lady and she will understand, I'm sure. I wish you hadn't published it, though. I have felt uneasy ever since it came out in print."

Rose remembered feeling the same thing when she realized it was too late to change her mind about publishing it and take it back. Now things were out of her hands. Her book had pushed them all into a situation that she had wanted to avoid. The job of informing Amey of her past and her power now fell to Jasper who would have to find a way to do both.

Lirin held up a hand to halt Rose's progress while he scanned the clearing ahead. They had been walking for over an hour and Rose leaned against the nearest tree to rest. Lirin hadn't gone by the most direct route to the lodge. The afternoon sun was high overhead and she was grateful for the shade of the trees. When Lirin turned to give the all clear, he saw that Rose needed a little more time. He passed the water bottle and pulled his pack off his back. He shared the fruit with Rose.

"We'll take a few minutes to rest," he said. "The Lodge is about fifteen minutes away but we want to be more careful as we approach. The Magician is searching everywhere for you and the Queen."

Choosing a soft bed of moss to sit on, Rose sat down to eat. She asked,

"Do you know if my mother is getting the support we will need?"

"The people are behind her, milady. The Magician hasn't made any friends with his cruelty and corruption."

"Do you hear anything about Prince Alair?

She hadn't meant to ask it but the question was one she felt compelled to ask. She needed to know.

"As far as anyone knows, milady, he is the same. Not many see him but those who have report that he looks healthy but...absent. He seems to exist in a daze. I'm sorry."

The sympathy in his voice brought tears to her eyes. She finished the fruit and got to her feet. Brushing herself off, she gave Lirin a small, embarrassed smile and said,

"Shall we?"

Lirin walked to the edge of the clearing to be sure it was safe to proceed. With respect for her feelings, he started off across the space. Rose followed wrapped in her thoughts.

It didn't take long before Rose could see the Lodge through the trees. It was a massive two-story log building with a dark grey slate roof. Huge timbers supported a porch and upstairs balcony that ran the full length of the broad front. Wings jutted out on both sides. It sat behind a living hedge with its rear side close in to the mountain. As at the farm, Bear Claw Mt. rose above the Lodge. This wasn't a fortified palace but was protected all the same. Powerful charged crystals and other gemstones were set to ward off discovery. Only those allowed to know where the Lodge was could get there.

The Lodge was a training center that was situated on the border between Freo and Altidio. Those found to be gifted in the use of gemstones in both kingdoms were brought here to study. It was used for this purpose even before Rose and her mother had to escape. Today it also served as headquarters for the campaign against the Magician. It sheltered those who were fugitives from his rule.

Lirin again stopped to listen carefully to the sounds around him. He looked in every direction then whistled a signal. It sounded like the trill of a bird but was answered immediately by another call. Satisfied that all was safe, Lirin led Rose through the hedge to the end of the porch. As they climbed the stairs, the front door burst open to release a tiny round woman who rushed forward to embrace Rose.

"Nanny? It is you! Oh, how wonderful to see you again!"

Rose held the jolly woman at arm's length and smiled happily. Her Mother had said nothing about her old nanny being at the Lodge. What a wonderful surprise. She loved this tiny woman who'd cared for her when she was a child but hadn't seen her since her escape. Nanny Pearl took her by the hand and led her to the door.

"Now you just come in here and let Nanny get you some tea. You look all tired out. You, young man, can come and get some too. Thank you for taking good care of my girl and getting her here to me safe and sound."

Lirin hid a smile and followed behind into the massive kitchen where Nanny Pearl had tea and cakes set out on the table by the window. She couldn't keep her hands from Rose- running a wrinkled hand over her hair, caressing her cheek. Her bright blue eyes were lost in her crinkled face as she smiled broadly. She finally sat down close to Rose and folded her arms on the table saying,

"Well now, young lady. Tell me everything!"

Rose laughed out loud.

"Everything, Nanny, would take too long! What are you doing here?"

"Your Mother found me and told me I had to come here. She wanted me safe. Who's going to want to hurt an old woman like me?"

"You know as well as I who would want to hurt you. Mother was right. The Magician would've loved to get his hands on you to use as a hostage. You are too important to us to allow that to happen. Do you know when Mother will be here?"

"She is staying with friends tonight and will be here tomorrow. She has her last meeting with community leaders tonight. Young man, what is your name again?"

"Lirin, ma'am."

"Of course, Jasper's nephew. Lirin, when you're finished there, can you go and tell the caretaker that Milady is here and to be sure that her room is ready?"

"Yes, ma'am. Thank you for the cake."

Lirin rose from the table and smiled when he thought what the headmaster would think of being called a caretaker. He left the two women chattering happily as they got to know each other again.

Later in her room, Rose prepared for bed. She'd spent the whole afternoon reminiscing with Nanny Pearl. Nanny fed her and coddled her. Rose shared her thoughts and fears with her just as she always had when she was a child and Nanny had somehow made her feel that everything was going to be fine.

The moon was shining through the window and Rose fell asleep.

Chapter Seven- The Journey

Amey woke first in the early morning when the sky was just beginning to brighten toward dawn. She was warm in her sleeping bag but knew that she wouldn't be able to sleep anymore. She hugged the bag close and thought about everything that she learned from Jasper the night before and the incredible experience of talking to her grandmother by the power of the stones. At least that's what she thought it must be. To tell the truth, she really didn't know what to think. The book, 'The Jewelled Kingdom,' that her mother had written had touched her when she read it as a remarkable story and she was proud of her. Her mother had wanted to know what Amey thought of it when she'd first given it to her to read and when she said she thought it was very good, her mother seemed to be waiting for something more. She hadn't understood at the time but she did now.

The story was romantic and tragic and Amey felt something tug inside her to realize that it was her family's story. She hadn't missed having a father when she was growing up because she'd never had one to miss. Now that she knew her father was alive, she wasn't sure what to think. Why hadn't her mother told her a long time ago? She had been raised to believe he had died before she was born. She guessed that was true – the man that he had been had been 'killed' in a way. What was he like? She vaguely remembered her mother saying that she looked just like her him.

Amey felt angry. No, not angry, really, but disappointed that her mother hadn't told her to her face rather than write it down in a book. Why? This was something that was important in her life. Wasn't it her right to know? She thought about her mother and realized something that she hadn't been aware of before. Her mother was always a little sad, it seemed. She would shy away when emotions ran high. Perhaps it was her way of grieving the loss of her previous life and her husband. It must've been so hard to be forced to flee leaving behind the man she loved and then find out you were going to have a baby. Her grandmother was there for her but she could grieve for her mother. That was all on Rose. Amey would leave this until she could talk to her Mom.

She was having a hard time, though, connecting the image of 'Queen Angeline' to her own grandmother. She pictured her in jeans and a pullover with a battered narrow-brimmed hat hauling a backpack with a bedroll and tools strapped to her back on their many hiking trips to dig up gemstones. She could see her scrambling over rocks, drinking directly from the spill of water falling over the rocks and dipping her face and arms in a pool of water at the end of a hot day to wash off the dirt of the trail. Or cooking the food they brought over a campfire. Her image of how a queen looked and acted was a long way from the many images she had of her grandmother! No, not exactly 'queenly'!

And her mother being a princess but married to a newly crowned king! Did that make her a queen too? Queen Rose! Wouldn't that make her a princess too? Oh, that was a good one! She wouldn't know the first thing about being a princess.

What she was having an even harder time with, though, was the idea of 'her power"! Jasper had walked her through a ritual that was similar to the rituals that her grandmother used to teach. Always, it involved mindfulness and being centred. She had spent many hours learning to clear her mind, concentrate on her breathing and then focus on the task at hand.

When she had been small, she had asked how they were able to get power from a stone and her grandmother's explanation had been that all power on earth came from God and, in God, all things were possible. Those who were trained could tap that energy and use it in many different ways. The power was neither good nor bad of itself but depended on the intentions of the one who was wielding it. At the time, Amey thought that she had understood but now, when she was to believe that she had a power to do wondrous things, she was having a lot more difficulty. She always assumed that it was God alone who did the deed not the person using the stone. But, in a way, that was also right.

She also remembered the first time that one of grandmother's rituals produced a result for her. They had found a baby bird that had fallen out of the nest. The day had been cold and the little bird had no warmth to its tiny body. It had been very near death and Amey had wanted her grandmother to help it. She instead had shown Amey how to use her crystal and how to enter into the power. The little bird began to warm and Amey was ecstatic. Its wings fluttered and it gradually sat up in her cupped hands. Soon it had fully recovered and she had replaced the bird in the nest. With pleasure, they had watched the mother return with food for her hungry babies not at all concerned that Amey had held one.

The pleasure of that memory warmed Amey's heart and turned her thinking to the possibility of her possessing a great power. It wasn't something she had ever considered. Now that she thought about the episode with the bird, she realized that she couldn't have done it without some power. It just came naturally to her, it seemed.

How would she use this power? What exactly could she do with her power? She turned her head to the side and looked across the dead fire to see Jasper quietly watching her.

"Good morning," he said.

There was a question in his voice but he said no more.

"Good morning."

She noticed that the sky was that lovely pale blue-grey one sees before the sun is fully above the horizon. She unfastened her bag, climbed out and headed for the cave entrance casting a quick shy glance over her shoulder at Jasper.

"Back soon," she said and headed around the rocks to answer nature's call. It was necessary to carry whatever you needed on a hike in one of your pockets or handy in your pack. She picked up a handful of snow and rubbed it over her hands then headed back into the cave. Jasper was up and had the fire started.

"Keep adding bigger pieces, will you?"

He also exited the cave to take his turn. Amey pulled over the bag with the supplies and opened it to see what was there. She took out another apple and bit in holding it in her mouth as she continued to search. There was a bag of pancake mix and a camp kit. Amey pulled these out also and set about mixing up a stiff batter using the water in the bottle. She bit off her piece of the apple and used the knife in the kit to cut up the rest of it to mix with the batter. There were some barbequing sticks leaning against the wall which were left there for the next person's use and Amey retrieved them. Sitting cross-legged before the cheery fire, Amey took some of stiff batter, rolled it in her palms and wrapped it in a spiral around one of the sticks. She wedged the stick between the rocks angling the batter over the flames. She then repeated the process with the second stick. As they cooked, she turned them to heat evenly.

Jasper returned with more firewood and put it on the pile in the back. He secretly smiled to see that Amey was reacting normally this morning. Earlier, he'd lain quietly watching her expressive face as thoughts raced through her mind. Her brow would crease then, as another thought would intrude, another expression would flit across her face. Just before she had turned to look across the fire pit, Jasper thought he saw a sort of acceptance and calm settle there.

"That smells good," he said and sat down on his sleeping bag.

He took out a small-lidded pot and added water from his bottle. Setting a flat rock against the inner ring of the fire pit, he set the pot of water there to boil. He dug in the bag again and brought out teabags. He looked up quickly at Amey before pulling out a bag of instant hot chocolate. When he held it out to her, her eyes opened wide with pleasure and she let out a little squeal.

"Hot chocolate! Oh, how wonderful!"

Passing him one of the sticks with the cooked batter, she gratefully took the metal cup he offered her and sat back to wait for the hot water. It didn't take long and they both enjoyed their breakfast in companionable silence.

When they were finished, Jasper set aside his cup and looked over the fire to Amey.

"Today we will be going to join your family. I have to teach you what to do so that you can perform the ritual for yourself. You will need to concentrate and let yourself open to the power of the stone. Picture yourself in the center of the power and embrace it- give yourself to it. When you are wholly committed, you use the same words that allowed you to speak to your grandmother but change the thought to travelling to your mother or Grandmother. Not having been there before means you have to just focus on them and going there. Only when you become one with the stone will you be able to go to them. This is a difficult thing to try to explain. We will just have to do it. I will help as much as I can but it is up to you. Do you understand, Amey?"

Amey tried to remember the feeling she experienced just before she spoke to her grandmother. She knew how to meditate and hoped that the discipline would be similar.

"Yes, Jasper, I think I do. I will try my best to learn the way."

Jasper searched her face with a slight frown between his brows which eased to an encouraging smile. Standing, he held out his hand and pulled Amey to her feet.

"I know you will. Let's gather our things and be on our way."

They packed up their belongings and hoisted the packs on their backs. They stepped out of the cave into a crisp, clear morning that promised to turn into a glorious day. After another quick smile, Jasper led the way back down the mountain. They walked through the dew-soaked forest for a short while and came upon the glade from behind. They stepped down over the rocks at the head of the stream and continued to the spot where Rose had stood the day before.

"OK, Amey. Take out your crystal. Close your eyes. Hold it in your right hand and bring it to the center of your chest. Feel the warmth of your body warm the stone. We're just going to relax now and breathe. Nice deep breaths. Concentrate on your breath. Feel it enter your lungs and feel it expelled. Be the breath as it moves. Once you are completely one with your breath, hold out your other hand, palm up, and repeat the simple prayer I taught you last night.

"By Your power I am empowered. Open the way for me."

"When you feel the power fill you, do not be afraid but embrace it as you did the breath. Become one with it. Can you feel the peace, Amey?"

As if from far away, Amey replied,

"Yes."

"Good. Now just keep doing as I say. Become one with the power of the stone. When you are ready, hold out your hand, repeat the prayer, and keep the thought in your mind 'I want to go to my family.' Let the energy expand to fill you and fulfill your will."

Jasper watched carefully and saw Amey relax and a peaceful softness come to her face. As if in a dream, she held out her hand palm up and repeated the prayer from the night before. She seemed to shimmer as in a heat haze and then she was gone. Jasper hastened to follow. Soon there was nothing but the soft, fresh morning in the glade.

The town was quiet and she saw no one about. Angeline cautiously approached the mayor's house and heard crying from inside. She knocked on the door while looking around for signs of danger. The door was wrenched open and the mayor's wife faced her with tears streaming down her face.

"Oh, Milady! You have to help! They've taken him away and hurt my boy! I don't know what to do to help him!"

She took Angeline's hand and pulled her into the house. Angeline stopped her to ask,

"Who took your husband, Anna?"

"It was that evil Magician and his men! They came here to find out where you were. They know you have a shelter around here, they said. They wanted my husband to tell them where. They said that, as he was the mayor, he would know where you were. Donal said he had no idea where you were. They wouldn't believe him and took him away. When my boy tried to stop them taking his Da, the Magician put his hand on his head. He just collapsed on the floor and I can't get him to wake up! When Donal fought to come back to help, one of his men knocked him out and dragged him away."

She pulled Angeline into the livingroom and over to the sofa where a boy of Galen's age lay supported by pillows. He was breathing but showed no other signs of life. Angeline placed her hand on his forehead. He had no fever. His body was limp and, under his eyelids, his eyes were rolled back in his head. This casual cruelty was just what Angeline expected of the Magician. With her hand on his head, she concentrated on the boy. After a few moments, she stood and turned to the mother.

"Anna, I don't know what I can do here. We must get him to the Lodge. Go get someone to carry him. By the way, where is everyone?"

"When the Magician left with Donal, some of the men followed through the woods to see where he went. They haven't come back yet. I think the women are hiding in their homes."

"I see. Go find someone who can carry your boy to the Lodge. Galen, take the horse and ride to the Lodge. Let them know what has happened here."

Galen ran out the door and untied the horse. He climbed on the fence to boost himself into the saddle and galloped off to deliver the message. Angeline crouched down by the boy and rested her hand on his forehead whispering a prayer. She hoped that Rose was at the Lodge. Even more, having Amey there would be the best. She clutched the crystal at her neck, sank into its power and let it flow into the boy. She didn't expect it to revive him but hoped to ease the fear she felt when she touched him. She rose when she heard running footsteps and turned to see the neighbour's teenage son come through the door. He bowed his head with a shy, "Milady" and went over to pick up the small boy. When he came over to Angeline's side, she put her hand on his forehead and sent her thoughts to his mind. He would now be able to find the way but would forget when the instructions faded.

"Take him quickly to the Lodge. I have sent a message on ahead of you so that they will be ready. I will follow on foot."

Anna was unsure what she should do with her boy going out the door but Angeline put her arm around her shoulder and said,

"Stay here in case your husband returns. I don't think the Magician will keep him long when he finds that he doesn't know where the Lodge is. He will need you here to tell him about your son. You can assure him that we will do everything to revive him. I will send a message back to you with information as soon as I can."

She put her arms around the shaken woman and held her offering comfort. She said a silent prayer and willed a healing calm to support her. When she felt her ease, she led her to a chair at the table. Taking the hot water off the stove, she made her a cup of chamomile tea. When she was settled, Angeline said goodbye, giving her assurance that she would keep her informed.

Outside again, Angeline didn't feel comfortable taking the road. She paused to set a ward around herself so that she couldn't be followed and stepped into the woods on the edge of the town. Keeping to the dense growth, she headed off in the direction of the Lodge. The boy would be there by now and Angeline hurried to catch up. She was seriously worried about the boy. She'd been blocked from reaching his mind. Rose was there at the Lodge by now. She hoped that their combined power could break through without harming him.

She hurried up the steps and entered the Lodge happy to find Rose and Nanny Pearl making the boy comfortable in one of the student's rooms off the kitchen. He was pale and appeared no better than before. Rose ran to her and hugged her close in welcome.

"Mother, what happened to him? The boy brought us a message that the Magician did something to him. Is that right?"

They watched as Nanny Pearl placed cool cloths on the boy's forehead and settled a soft blanket over his limp form.

"Yes. When the boy went to stop them taking his father away, the Magician put his hand on his head and he just collapsed. I couldn't reach his mind. There's something blocking the way. I thought together we might do more. I don't even know his name."

From behind came the voice of the young man who had carried him. He was standing by the wall with Lirin.

"His name is Perrin, milady. He's only seven."

Angeline went to him and took his hand.

"We will do all that we can. What's your name?"

"My name is Doan, milady."

"Well, Doan, I want you to go into the kitchen and wait there for us. Nanny Pearl? Will you make Doan a tea and give him a snack?"

"Of course. Come along, young man. Let's see what we can get you and let these ladies do what they can for the boy."

Rose and Angeline stood together trying to decide what to do. They both lifted their heads when they heard the whistle and knew what it meant. Together they said,

"Amey" and hurried from the room.

Chapter Eight - Reunion

Amey stood in the clearing looking around in amazement. What an incredible experience! She found she still had her hand out and her crystal clenched to her chest. Putting it back in her bag, she looked up to find Jasper standing in front of her.

"Jasper! That was incredible!"

Jasper smiled at the wonder on her face. He watched as she looked around the glade waiting to see her reaction. When he saw where she was looking, he said,

"The one thing that amazed us when we went to the farm was the fact that the same mountain was there too. Your Grandmother traveled all over that world and found other similar places and features."

Amey gazed at the mountain that held so much meaning for her. If she had been asked what she would miss the most in leaving, it would've been Bear Claw Mt. She studied her surroundings more carefully. The trees and plants around her looked just like those she left behind. The singing of the birds and other forest sounds felt familiar. The scent of the air- all the same!

"Everything is so similar here, Jasper. Will I notice a great deal of differences?"

"Yes, you will. Time has slowed development here and there is no electricity or phones. People live a more rustic life with few amenities. Travel here is still by horse, wagon and carriage or by foot. Think back to the stories of the early 19th century. You will also notice that the people speak more formally. For instance, your mother and grandmother are addressed as 'milady' as a form of respect."

"Why didn't you bring back the technology from home to here? Surely it would've made life easier for the people?"

"Technology doesn't always translate to happiness. Life here is simple, or, at least, it was before the Magician took over. Most things are still done by hand although we have been slowly bringing in advancements. I know that the queen has decided that change has to be slow and well thought out. You'll have to have this discussion with your grandmother about technology. She will explain her reasons better than I can."

Amey stood taking everything in. Jasper wanted to start for the Lodge but gave her some extra time to adjust. The first experience traversing dimensions can be disorienting but Amey didn't appear to be affected at all.

"Come on, Amey. We need to get to the Lodge and we have to be careful. The Magician has agents everywhere and we don't want to bring their attention to our whereabouts. There are safe-guards that deter anyone from crossing the warded perimeter but the Magician would only need to know the vicinity to be able to find us. We have prevented that by misdirecting his men around the location and they are never the wiser."

They entered the forest along the same path that Rose and Lirin had the day before. Amey was fascinated that everything seemed the same. Her mountain loomed over them and the trees and foliage were exactly the same. She followed the brisk pace Jasper set easily. The trees here even appeared to be the same age as the ones at the farm and the hike made Amey feel right at home. They didn't stop to rest and reached the Lodge in just over an hour.

Jasper gave a whistle before he approached the Lodge and received one in answer. He still waited until he was assured there was no one in the vicinity and then led Amey up the stairs to the porch where they entered the enormous common room. Rushing to greet them were both Angeline and Rose. Rose hugged her daughter with relief while Angeline smiled a welcome.

"You're finally here. I'm so sorry about all this. It's all my fault that we're on the run. I should never have published that book!"

Angeline touched Rose's shoulder and pulled her away. She was also glad to see Amey but there were more important matters at hand.

"Welcome, Amey. You've been through so much already but I'm afraid we need your help now. We have a little boy here who the Magician touched and we can't bring him back."

She put her hands on either side of Amey's face and looked into her eyes.

"Jasper told you more about your ability. I believe you have the power to help him. I know you don't believe in it fully yet, but I need you to try. He needs you to try. Can you do this? Will you try?"

It was all happening too fast. All the revelations and amazing experiences were too much to take in. Amey felt panic beginning to build. She didn't know anything. How was she supposed to help a little boy touched by evil magic? Healing a little bird didn't qualify her for this kind of request! She looked frantically from face to face.

"Amey, please, you have to try. He's only a little boy and we have to reverse the evil that the Magician has done. Can you do this for him? Will you try, please? I am confident that you have the talent to do this"

She looked around blankly and her eyes met confident vivid green ones which smiled understandingly at her. Lirin calmly held her gaze and said,

"You can do this. I know you can. Will you try?"

The panic began to subside somewhat. Amey drew in strength from those around her. She looked into her grandmother's concerned eyes, and then her mother's. She nodded her head.

"Yes, I will try. But you have to help me because I don't know what to do."

They returned to the boy's room and Amey saw the small body lying there so still. Angeline said,

"Amey, remember when you revived the baby bird? What you did there is something like what's needed here. With the bird, you called on its will to live and it did. Use your crystal to focus your power. Trust in your strength. There is something blocking his mind. I can't reach him. You need to go in gently and try to break through the barrier. You have to be very cautious. His name is Perrin. Call to him with your mind and gently push your way through to him."

Amey nodded. She looked at the small body lying there looking lifeless but for the breathing. The enormity of what they were asking her to do started to well up in her but she pushed it back down. She took a chair and sat down in front of the boy. She removed her crystal from her bag and took a deep breath. She thought back to the night before and Jasper helping her contact her grandmother. She remembered how Jasper walked her through the ritual. She squared her shoulder and sought a meditative state. She consciously controlled her breathing in a measured way. She continued to breathe, following the breath as it traveled through her body. She felt the peace enfold her. Taking the crystal in her hands, she closed her eyes and breathed deeply and evenly. She continued to concentrate on her breath and felt the powerful pull of the crystal. She went toward the power and sank into it. She lifted the crystal to her forehead with one hand and reached to touch the boy's forehead with the other. The crystal glowed in her mind with a clear white light that grew in intensity. Amey urged the Light outward and reached for the boy. She felt the Light moving down her arm and into the boy. But it stopped there. Amey could feel the barricade like a physical wall. Amey called to the boy in her mind.

"Perrin. I'm here to help you. Reach out to me."

Amey sought to strengthen the Light. Once again, she moved the Light forward and felt a slight give but still it held. Amey offered up the simple prayer Jasper had taught her.

"By your power, I am empowered. Help me."

This time when she advanced the light, she felt the obstruction give way a little. She could see into the boy's mind and shuddered at the picture there. The slavering beasts tearing apart his mother and father. Running to hide as far away as he could and making no sound to attract the beast that was destroying everything around it as it searches for him. It played over and over in his mind. The Magician had done this! It enraged her and she gave herself over to the light.

"By your power, I am empowered. Help me."

With all her concentration, Amey sought to erase the image from the boy's mind. It began to dissolve like ink on wet paper gradually fading to nothing.

"Perrin. Reach out to me. Nothing is going to harm you. I have removed the evil thing and you are safe. Reach out to me"

Perrin responded and reached out to her. With that motion, the final barricade came down and he fell into an easy sleep with a peaceful smile on his face. Amey smoothed away any remaining disquiet and eased away. She withdrew the light from Perrin and let it absorb into her body. She felt alive from the light. When she no longer felt the crackle of power, she opened her eyes.

No one spoke. Amey stood up and turned around to find everyone staring at her in amazement.

"I've never seen anything like that before."

Jasper spoke before all the others. It broke them out of their stupor and they all began to talk at once.

"I knew you could do it," said her grandmother.

"Oh, Amey," was all her mother could say.

From a very different voice came a simple,

"Well done."

Amey broke into a big smile. She felt as light as a feather.

"Amey, you now have to believe what we've been telling you. You have an incredible power. What you did here is beyond anything I've ever seen. While we watched, your body began to glow. Your arm that touched the boy had a stream of light running down it. We all felt the barricade come down. What can I say? I'm so proud of you!"

Her grandmother's words amazed Amey. She thought that the light was only in her mind but they saw it too!

Amey looked back at the boy. "He is peaceful now. The Magician had placed horrible images in his mind so that he was hiding in fear and couldn't come out on his own."

"Amey, what can we do for you? Would you like anything?"

Her mother's concern touched her and she wrapped her in her arms giving her a big hug.

"I'm hungry. Is there anything to eat?"

Everyone laughed in relief and headed to the kitchen. The boy would now sleep easily. They would let him rest for a while before returning him to his family. Amey met the young man with the green eyes in the doorway. He stood aside to allow her to pass.

"By the way, I'm Lirin."

"Nice to meet you, Lirin, I'm Amey. Thank you"

Together they went to see what Nanny Pearl had by way of food.

They were a congenial group around the large kitchen table. Everyone spoke of what they had experienced and questions flew back and forth. Nanny Pearl had produced an amazing amount of food on such short notice and everyone enjoyed the bounty.

"Nanny Pearl? I want you to meet my daughter Amey. Amey, Nanny Pearl was my nanny for as long as I can remember." Rose happily introduced her daughter to her former nanny.

Nanny Pearl was very interested in the daughter of her former charge. She looked intently at Amey, touching her cheek, and running her wrinkled hand softly over her dark hair. She seemed to come to some satisfactory conclusion and put her arms around both Amey and Rose. With a happy chuckle she said,

"Now I have two little ones to take care of. Let's get you settled. You both look like you could use a little care."

She served everyone but hovered over Rose and Amey offering them extra special attention. Angeline looked on with a smile. They would need all the care they could get before they faced what was to come.

Chapter Nine- Contemplation

Perrin awoke showing no apparent sign of ill effects. He was surprised not to be at home and shy to be among such important people. When Angeline gently questioned him over cake and herbal tea, he said he must've had a bad dream but he couldn't remember what it was. She touched his head tousling his hair in order to search his mind for any harmful aftereffects. She was pleased to find him without consequences from his encounter with the Magician. Doan was sent to bring him home accompanied by Jasper and Lirin. If the mayor had been returned and uninjured, they would bring him back to the Lodge. Angeline needed any information he might have. When Jasper returned, he reported the mayor would come the next day as he was still being treated for his injuries.

"He was bruised and battered but otherwise unharmed. Donal and Anna were grateful to have their boy back safely and he promised that he would be here. Lirin will go get him in the morning. He's lucky he had no knowledge to offer up otherwise I don't think he would be alive now."

The food had been removed and they were discussing the future.

"I agree. We need to get started quickly. The Magician is stepping up his searches and I don't want the support we have now being subverted. We have Rose here and, most important, we have Amey. I knew when she was little that she possessed extraordinary power but I had no idea of the extent even as untrained as she is. It will give us a great advantage."

Angeline gave Amey an encouraging smile.

"We need to determine just what you are capable of doing. You have to be the one to rescue your father. Your ability with the mind of the child tells me that you are best suited to help him. Being your father, you will have that much more incentive. We know that he seems to be in a trance and that means some form of mind control is being used. To our benefit, the Magician doesn't know about you."

Jasper turned to Rose and asked,

"Rose, you will need to write down everything that you can remember about Alair's palace. Draw up a map and accurate floor plan so that we can study it and familiarize ourselves with the layout. Lirin tells me that there are many of the Magician's men not very far from here. With the wards on the Lodge, they shouldn't be able find it but it might be a good idea to make them think we are somewhere else."

Lirin leaned in and spread out a map on the table.

"We will put together a little diversion and make them think they discovered our headquarters. They will think they just missed us. We can have it appear that we scattered to find another safe place"

"Good. Good. A diversion will give us a little extra time to plan. Amey will need to know everything that we can tell her about Altidio and Freo. Her power will do no good if she can't get to where she is needed most."

Amey listened to her grandmother, Jasper and all the others as they spoke of the plans to confront the Magician. She was uneasy to hear how much was expected of her and her newfound power. She had barely gotten used to the idea of having a power and now she was expected to use it to defeat a Magician. Use it against a Magician who could entrap a mind in horror as he had so easily done to small Perrin. The exhilaration of the moment with Perrin had worn away leaving an uneasy nervousness.

What grandmother had taught to her when she was a little girl had seemed like a game to her. It had been fun to hold a gemstone in her hands, say some words and make things happen. All the little rituals appealed to her sense of wonder and imagination. Her friends at school weren't interested in her 'magic tricks' so she had kept them to herself. She knew that they just didn't understand and her grandmother advised her not to try.

This, however, was something else- something out of fairy tales right down to the evil Magician! Just yesterday, she had been reading 'The Jewelled Kingdom.' She had enjoyed the exciting, sad story between the pages of the book and now she was in the book! She was at the center of the conflict of good against evil and expected to be the one to 'slay the dragon,' so to speak.

Lirin cast a sidelong glance in Amey's direction noticing her agitation. As he watched, she got up quietly from the table and went to the door that led out to the covered porch. She quietly slipped out into the half-light of the late afternoon. As he watched through the window, Amey set her hip on the rail and leaned back against the post. There was tension in every line of her face and body.

Lirin eased away from the conversation that flowed over the table. No one observed his departure and he went through the same door to join Amey on the porch. She watched him approach and gave him a tentative smile.

"A little overwhelming for you, isn't it?"

He sat across from her against the opposite post looking away from her troubled face to watch the last rays of the sun light the yard. This was a lot to dump on an unsuspecting person and he wanted to help ease her into it.

"I've lived this conflict all my life, Amey. Everything I do is in preparation for the day we defeat the Magician. From the time I was born, I worked for this day. The Magician killed my father when he resisted telling where Queen Angeline and Rose were. He was her Chief Steward and had helped them escape here to the Lodge after the Magician came to destroy their palace. Jasper took them away to safety and then came back to scout out the situation. He brought me to the shelter of the Lodge and I have lived here ever since preparing for the final conflict.

"My father was Jasper's only brother. When he was alive, we lived in a house on the palace grounds after my mother died. I was there when the Magician came and tried to force his will on my father's mind to get information. He had enough control to resist but the effort stopped his heart. I was three years old and watched from the hiding place my father had shown to me. After they ransacked the palace destroying everything and left my father just lying there tied to the chair, Jasper came. He knew where to find me and took my hand to lead me out. He was in tears as he cut the bonds that bound my father. He carried him to a rear entrance where he had a wagon, put my father in it and me on the seat beside him and drove us away from there to the Lodge. There was nothing left to go back to so this has been my home ever since. My father is buried over there under that lilac tree."

Amey swallowed the tears in her throat and said in a quiet voice,

"I'm so sorry, Lirin. You have suffered so much. I'm embarrassed to be so scared. I have never had anything bad happen to me. I've been cared for all my life and enjoyed the company of both my mother and grandmother. We lived a quiet life on the farm. I learned to ride horses and my grandmother and I spent hours exploring Bear Claw Mountain. That's where grandmother and I collected our gemstones. Sometimes mother would come too but mostly it was only my grandmother and me. We used to sit by the stream in the glade-you know- our glade? That's where grandmother would teach me about the stones. I learned all their properties and some of the rituals and prayers but I had no idea of the extent of their power. It all seemed just like fun and games to me."

Amey paused and looked out at the mountain.

"Do you know what I was looking forward to most when I got home on vacation? I couldn't wait to climb up Bear Claw Mt. I've spent many happy hours and days roaming over that mountain. I don't know what it is about it that draws me so much. I just know that it does.

'My mother wrote the story of 'The Jewelled Kingdom' and had it published. That's how the Magician found us. She gave it to me to read. It seemed like a wonderful sad fairy tale with no happy ending.

I didn't know it was real until yesterday when Jasper saved me from being captured by the Magician. I knew nothing of this kind of power. What I learned as a child was to recognize the stones and their powers, heal little creatures, and ease a headache. How am I supposed to fight against a Magician? I don't know anything!"

Lirin understood her fear but he knew what he's seen her do with the boy. He sought to find the right words to comfort her.

"Amey, what I saw you do today I've never seen anyone do. You, without any training, broke the hold the Magician had over Perrin's mind. You instinctively knew what to do. What you were taught as a child was basic control. You were able to use that knowledge to counteract the Magician's powerful spell. I don't think your grandmother or mother could've done more with all the years of training and practice that they've had. I have some power myself and couldn't imagine doing that. Do not doubt yourself so much."

Amey's brows drew together in a frown.

"What he had done made me so angry! I don't understand how anyone can do something so cruel," she said.

Amey thought about what Lirin said before. He stirred a question that had occurred to her when she had traveled with Jasper.

"Lirin, does everyone here have powers? Jasper taught me what to do so that I could come here but he didn't tell me too much more."

Lirin smiled and explained at Amey's confused expression.

"Not everyone in Altidio and Freo have powers nor does everyone who does have power wish to use it. Those who do use it, have aptitudes in different areas and to varying degrees. Jasper could show you what to do because he instructs those who have the talent in their use and development. Back when I was a boy, Jasper ran this training facility-that's what the Lodge was originally. All the people who showed a talent and were eager were brought here for training. He will not let you go into this unprepared. I'm sure he already has something planned."

Lirin's words gave her some comfort. She looked back out to the mountains and sighed.

"I wish I could go, for just a little while, and climb up the mountain and find my balance. I seem to be unsteady and the mountain always brought me peace."

"Then we will try to find some time to do just that. I promise. I will be busy for the next couple of days, but after that I might be able to arrange it for you. If you work hard at your lessons, Jasper won't object to having some time off."

"That would be wonderful! Thank you, Lirin."

She looked over when the door opened again and her mother came out to join them. She was concerned about Amey. She's been so focused on talking about possibilities with her mother that she hadn't seen Amey leave. So much had been thrown at her in such a short while. Lirin stood at her approach and said a simple "goodnight" leaving them alone together. Rose searched her daughter's face.

"How are you holding up, Amey? Are you alright? I feel so guilty for messing everything up so bad. Just recently I realized that part of the reason I delayed was because it was too painful. I wish I had told you sooner instead of writing that book! I was so absorbed in my grief that I couldn't bring myself to tell you. I was afraid that I couldn't say the words and that I wouldn't know how to explain. Then I was afraid that you would be angry because I left it so long to tell you. I still miss your father so much!"

Amey could see the uncertainty there and felt an answering concern for her mother.

"I'm fine. A little overwhelmed, for sure, but fine. I know it was hard for you to tell me. It is a fantastic story. But I'm a big girl now, Mother, and I would've understood. You should've told me everything sooner. I always knew there was something in the background. You often seemed so sad. Grandmother would start to say things and then stop. So would you. It's good to know. How much of "The Jewelled Kingdom" is exactly as it was?"

Rose blushed and looked at Amey with an embarrassed smile.

"All of it. I used my diary and just copied everything down. I'm not actually that good of a writer. The story itself was what sold the book. The critic praised the 'imagination" if not the writing. I didn't know that the Magician could travel through space like we could. Your father's family doesn't control the stones. I underestimated him and that was a big mistake."

"Will Jasper be able to teach me what to do?"

"Amey, we will all teach you what you need to know. It's been a long day and Jasper wants to start tomorrow. We are putting a lot on your young shoulders. Grandmother is sure you will stand up to it but I think we should go a little slower. We will see. Now, let's make an early night of it and get off to bed. After all this excitement, it will be a wonder if we can go to sleep at all."

They went in arm-in-arm and headed upstairs saying 'good night' as they went. They were sharing the big room with twin beds that faced into the yard where Rose slept the night before. Nanny Pearl had the same thought about them having trouble going to sleep and brought up two cups of warm milk. She tucked both of them in and gave them each a kiss on the cheek.

"You two sleep well now. Tomorrow's problems will still be there to solve tomorrow. Good night."

"Good night, Nanny Pearl" they both responded.

Once Nanny Pearl was gone, Amey crept out of bed and climbed in with her mother.

"Tell me all about my father, please?"

Rose smiled in the darkness. It was just like when Amey was little and wanted to hear a story. Then too she would climb in bed and ask for whatever story took her interest.

"I met your father when he came with his parents on an official state visit. That sounds so stuffy! Actually, they were very good friends with your grandparents and my father before he died in an epidemic that killed many people in both countries. Alair and I hadn't met since we were small. Either I was away or he was when visits were arranged. Anyway, this time both of us were there. He was beautiful! Not quite the word, I guess, but he was. He had shoulder length hair that waved-just like yours does. His eyes were a deep blue and he was tanned from being outdoors so much. I think I fell in love with him the first time I looked at him.

While our parents talked, we walked in the garden. We talked and talked. It was as if we had known each other forever! He liked the things I liked. I was interested in similar things that he was interested in. It was amazing! After that first visit, he made all sorts of excuses to come and see me. I think both of our parents were amused.

Alair had to do some travelling on state business for his father and was away for several months. During that time, my father took sick and died. My Mother and I couldn't help him. We were devastated. Alair's parents offered their condolences but I think they advised him to give us time to grieve. Mother buried her grief under her obligation as Queen to the people. They supported her fully and she drew great comfort from it."

Rose paused as she remembered that sad time and how strong her mother had been.

"Alair waited through the mourning period, but, as soon as it was over, he came to visit. I hadn't been as strong as my mother had and took my father's death hard. When Alair came, though, it was as if a weight was lifted from me. I could breathe again. He asked me to marry him and I said yes. Not right away, because of my father's recent death, but as soon as possible. Both families were happy for us and plans were made."

Rose rubbed Amey's arms as she held her.

"Amey, your father is a good and decent man. He cared for people. He loved his parents and he loved me. We were so happy. We were planning for the future. We wanted to have children. Oh, Amey, you looked so much like him when you were little! It was both a pleasure and a pain to have you resemble him so much. It reminded me of what I had lost. But it also gave me the comfort of having something of him that I could hold close and love."

Amey felt strangely comforted. She also felt a firm resolve.

"We will get him back. I promise you that I will do everything I can to make it happen. Thank you for telling me. I feel closer to him now."

She snuggled into her mother's arms and held her close. They each felt content and drifted off to sleep with no bad dreams to interrupt their rest.

Chapter Ten – Training

Lirin had been right. Jasper had the morning planned out. He was there at the breakfast table impatient to get to work. Angeline had to lead him to his seat, pour him a cup of tea, and get him to eat some food in order for Amey to be able to finish hers. He wasn't deterred for long, though, and Amey found herself whisked off to start her lessons as soon as she finished. It was a beautiful, warm morning and Jasper led her to a sunny garden where there were seats set around a small, rustic table. More seating was tucked away in various location around different features like a pond and a knot garden. The location was beautiful. It merged seamlessly with the surrounding woods. The basic framework featured shaped evergreens and shrubs that were just leafing out in wonderful shades of green, copper and russet. There was an arbor that was completely covered with a vine but wasn't in leaf as yet. This led into a larger garden that looked to be the kitchen garden. The ground had been freshly turned and made into rows ready for planting. Everything was just as it would be back at the farm.

Amey was pleased to see her mountain towering above the treetops. She thought Jasper might've chosen this place to give her something familiar after all the strangeness. Before they started, he took out a velvet bag and removed a necklace. It had a fine golden chain and a large crystal in the shape of a teardrop suspended from it. He gave it to her to put on.

"This is from your grandmother. It is a pure, blemish free crystal of singular power. It will be easier for you to work without having to carry one in a bag. Having one on your person gives you more freedom to react. She had this made for you in anticipation of this time."

Amey held it in her hand and watched the sunlight fracture on its faceted surface. It was stunning in its clarity. She could feel it warm to her hand and released it to let it lie on her shirtfront.

"I will be teaching you how to explore your power- see some of what it can or cannot do. We already know a little bit of what you can do after yesterday. You have an instinctive knowledge but you need to be able to use it in times of crisis. I will lead you along that path. We are cramming years of study into a short period of time. Use everything you have been taught before and figure out what will work best for you. It isn't the same for everyone. I have a great confidence in you. Now, let's get started."

Jasper led her through all the small rituals that her grandmother had taught her. He studied her technique minutely and showed her new ones that might work better for her. They explored her knowledge of various gemstones and their application. He lifted a leather case onto the table and opened it to reveal an interior divided into smaller velvet-lined sections each holding a different gemstone. Pulling on tabs on the side, he lifted that layer out revealing another also filled with more gemstones. It was a truly dazzling display as the sun caused the various stone to glow or shimmer in its rays.

"You will need these as well as your crystal to help your father. The Magician has had control over him for a long time and you will need to choose which stones will work best when you are able to assess him. We will work out possible scenarios a little later."

For the next hour, Jasper tested her knowledge of the stones in front of her making sure she understood fully what they were and for what they could be used. He chose stones at random and had Amey hold them to feel the residual power in each and to see if she could activate them. He had Amey perform some of the simple rituals to see how she worked and corrected a few of her methods to improve her efficiency.

"Simple is best. When you're in danger, longer rituals are easier to forget. When you have the time, use the intricate ones. They will give you more control and focus your power better."

Mid-morning, Nanny Pearl marched out carrying refreshments. By the determined look in her eye, Jasper realized it was useless to argue. She set down a tray with fruit, cookies, tea with milk, and even a coffee for Jasper.

"All that thought work needs fuel. Don't you go working this little girl too hard on her first day, Jasper. She won't be any good to anyone if you wear her out."

She stayed to make sure that they ate and drank to her approval then went back to the Lodge. Jasper waited until she was out of hearing and said,

"She's been like that for as long as I can remember. Even when I had grown into a man, she treated me like I was just out of diapers. Now it's your turn. You're her new baby to care for and spoil."

He grinned at her and, when Amey smiled back, she realized that she had been wound up tight with tension and made an effort to relax. Jasper watched her with approval. He knew that he was pushing her faster than was ideal but there wasn't much time to waste. He would have to be very aware of Amey's emotional state and try to ease up when he could. Lirin told him the night before that Amey wanted to go up on the mountain to centre herself and that he would arrange it in a couple of days. Jasper knew what the mountain meant to Amey and was thankful that Lirin was befriending Amey and recognized the need in her.

"You need to keep yourself stress-free and calm. Meditation is the best thing for that. Keep up with it. Anytime you feel stressed, if you can, close your eyes for a moment and listen to your breath. It always helps. It takes you back to basics."

They resumed the lesson and Jasper had her try new things. He wanted to introduce actions that could be applied in their coming quest but make them more fun to do. He put a leaf on the table and directed Amey to move it with her mind. She looked at him as if he were joking. He showed her how to do it by concentrating his mind on the thought of moving the leaf. It moved around the table as if a breeze were swirling it around. Amey smiled in delight.

"Relax and go into yourself. Think of the leaf. See it in detail. Concentrate on the idea of moving it across the table. Think back to how you moved yourself here."

Amey looked at the leaf, saw its detail and form and concentrated her mind on the thought of moving the leaf. It didn't move, didn't even flutter. She looked up at Jasper in disappointment.

"See it in your mind moving across the table. Press your mind down onto the leaf and use your thoughts like you would your finger."

She again focused on the leaf and felt its texture. She pictured putting pressure on the leaf and pushing. Without breaking that contact, she pushed her thoughts against the surface of the leaf and happily saw it moving slowly across the table and jumped when it did. She laughed in surprise.

"I did it! Did you see it move? I did it!"

"Yes, you did. Good work. What did you feel when it moved?"

The question surprised her. She thought back to the moment when the leaf moved. How had she felt?

"I felt focused and peaceful. Until it moved and then I was startled."

"That peacefulness is the power working through you. When you accomplish a task, you have to maintain that peacefulness so that you don't undermine what you've accomplished. You need to expect what you are trying to do will happen so that you don't lose focus."

Jasper had her do it over and over until it came easily then switched to a pebble. Amey found that the process was the same but that she had to absorb the difference in the stone's structure in relation to the leaf. She worked at moving the heavier pebble and found that it came easier this time. Jasper was pleased with her progress. They tried other exercises that tested her ability and put a determined glint in her eyes.

By noon, Jasper wasn't as worried as he'd been in the morning. They broke for lunch and Jasper said,

"When we come back after lunch, I want to teach you some things that can save your life and others. It is a hard lesson and I don't expect you to get it immediately, so, don't be upset if you can't. Now, go and relax and let Nanny Pearl take care of you."

He left her at the porch stairs and walked away toward the student quarters. Amey went into the kitchen and crossed to the table where her grandmother and mother were eating soup. Nanny Pearl saw her and immediately filled a bowl and brought it to the table.

"I was just coming out to get you, my girl. You mustn't miss your meals. You have a lot of growing to do yet and you need good food for that. Sit yourself down and I will bring over the sandwiches and tea."

Amey smiled her thanks. She didn't realize she was hungry until she smelled the aroma of the fragrant bowl in front of her. Apparently, her grandmother and mother thought the same. No one spoke until they were finished.

"That was delicious. I forgot how good a good cook Nanny Pearl is."

Rose put down her napkin and looked enquiringly at her daughter.

"How was your morning, dear?"

"Amazing and tiring! Jasper said he was pleased with my progress. When we started this morning, he was tense and now he seems more relaxed. He wants to show me how to defend myself after lunch."

She reached into her shirt and pulled out the crystal.

"Thank you for this crystal, Grandmother. It is so beautiful."

"It is also very powerful. I found the stone in a bazaar on one of my trips. I want you to have all the help you need."

Rose seemed concerned.

"Do you think Jasper is pushing her too hard, Mother? She's just barely arrived and she's being asked to do so much."

"Rose, everyone is being asked to do a lot. We don't have a lot of time. Do you feel overwhelmed, Amey?"

Amey didn't reply right away. How did she feel? She remembered the night before on the porch but didn't think she felt quite that same way today. The work with Jasper had a lot to do with it. She didn't feel so helpless and Jasper was going to teach her to protect herself and others in the afternoon. She realized that, just as in the ritual invocation, she was feeling empowered. She still feared the future but thought she could cope.

"I'm afraid but I know how important this is and I feel stronger after working with Jasper. I still find all this hard to believe. It's like I'm dreaming. Everything has happened so fast that there's been no time to take it in properly."

Angeline looked at her granddaughter with sympathy. She squeezed the hand resting on the table.

"I know this has been hard for you but I want you to know I'm very proud of you for the way you've adjusted. No one wanted to have things turn out this way for you. Remember, if you need it, all or any one of this group will be there to help you. Don't be afraid we will think badly of you. If it gets too much, have yourself a good cry or a scream and get it out of your system. We love you so much and we are afraid also. "Not to fear is to be a fool." I don't remember who said that but it is true."

They were interrupted when Nanny Pearl came back to the table to see how they were doing. She gathered their plates to the side and poured more tea for Angeline and Rose. She knew they were worried and went to Amey, smoothing her hair away from her face.

"You are a good and clever girl. Jasper will teach you well and everything will be OK. But now I have something to show you."

She went to the sideboard and retrieved a small parcel wrapped in a soft cloth.

Placing it on the table in from of Amey, she began to unwrap it , pushing aside the edges to reveal an oval picture frame. Turning it over, Nanny Pearl said,

"When your grandmother had me brought here for safety, I gathered together all my belongings and other precious mementos of the family. I remembered last night that I had packed this away to give to your mother. She and your grandmother fled so quickly that they had no time to take anything. I think this should be for you."

She took away the wrapping and Amey was looking down at a small portrait of a couple on their wedding day. The artist had captured a tender moment between the two and Amey looked up at her mother as she traced the images.

"Is this you and my father?" she said with a hitch in her voice.

Rose came around the table and leaned down so that she could look also. There was wonder and sadness in her eyes as she looked from the portrait to her beloved Nanny.

'You saved this? Oh Nanny, you saved this for me? I've only had my memories of his face for all these years!" She hugged Amey and said in a soft voice,

"Yes, Amey, this is your father and I. The portrait was only finished just before we had to run. I don't think I even had time to study it before. The artist did a good job as he portrayed your father just as I remember him."

Amey studied the man in the portrait more closely. This man was her father in his wedding finery. It was clear how much he loved his new wife and the artist had caught the love and happiness in the eyes. He was tall and erect with broad shoulders and his black hair shone in the light. Her mother looked the same then as today only the happiness of the portrait was absent and there was a hint of sadness in her eyes as she looked at the painted image of her husband's face. The love and loss showed clearly.

"Nanny Pearl, thank you for giving this to me. It has been hard to get my head around having a father but this portrait gives me something tangible to focus on. You have made him more real and I now have something to work toward as an end goal. I will free my father!'

Amey stood up from the table and gave her a quick hug. Nanny Pearl looked on with concern in her eyes as Amey went out the door. Angeline and Rose shared a moment and the Rose picked up the portrait and also gave Nanny Pearl a hug.

"You have also given me a clear reason to fight. We loved each other and we made that lovely, brave girl. I can only do the same and fight for what was taken."

Jasper was met with a very determined girl when he returned to start the afternoon lessons. He didn't know what put the challenge in her eye but he could see clearly that Amey was wholly engaged. They started out simply again with meditation exercises. He wanted Amey to be able to enter the proper state with ease. What he had seen of Amey's ability so far made him think it wouldn't be too hard for her. Though she was untrained, she had great instincts. He was still amazed at what she'd accomplished with Perrin.

They worked on her meditation technique for a while until Jasper was satisfied with her ease of transition. She took instruction well and performed each assignment with relish. He then led her into more advanced levels.

"Amey, what did you experience yesterday?"

Amey thought back to her experience.

"I closed my eyes and reached for the power of the crystal. When I felt its pull, I saw a white light that got brighter and brighter. I used that Light to reach out to Perrin. But I felt a wall blocking me from reaching his mind. I tried to strengthen the Light and called out to the boy to reach out to me. I could feel the barricade give way a bit. It was then that I could see what had been put in his mind and I was angry.

I reached for more power and said the prayer you taught me and the barricade just dissolved."

Jasper considered everything she'd told him. He wasn't overly concerned that it was anger that strengthen the power to take down the barricade but he wanted to address the need for control and discarding emotion.

"Every time you call on your ability, you need to do it with pureness of thought. You said what you saw made you angry. And your anger was justified by the wickedness but you need to put aside all those emotions and focus on the power of your thought. You need to be in control of yourself so that you can be in control of your gift. If you let any powerful emotion like hate or fear or anger control you, you will not be in control of your power. Do you understand?"

Amey considered what he had said. She could see that if she was in the control of a powerful emotion, she could not properly control what needed to be done. But she didn't know how to stop the feeling.

"I understand the need, Jasper, but I don't understand how to shut off the emotions."

"You don't need to shut them off only be in control so that they do not affect what you are trying to do. We will continue with you on control issues but I want to move on to defense now. Relax now and centre yourself"

He thought she might be ready.

"I want to teach you to protect yourself. When you control the power of the stones, you can create a shield around yourself which will enable you to escape injury. If you are strong enough, you can extend that protection to others. Think of it as pulling an impenetrable dome over yourself and others. This requires you to be able to go quickly to where your power lies, embrace it and use it to do what you need done. When we go to confront the Magician, we will be actively in enemy territory most of the time. It is important for you to be able to achieve a protective state immediately if you are challenged. Your life and maybe other lives will depend on it."

Jasper hoped he wasn't scaring her. He knew she wasn't a frivolous person and could only pray that she was mature enough to be able to understand.

"Are you ready? Let's begin. I want you to clear your mind and relax. When you are relaxed and in a true meditative state, I want to you focus on reaching into the light just as you did with the boy. Relax and see the light. See it grow bright. Feel it drawing you to it. Once you are in the light, grasp the crystal and concentrate on the power you feel in the stone. When you feel it strongly, let yourself sink into that power. What you did with Perrin was call on the Light. I want you to do that again."

Amey cleared her mind and relaxed. She felt the peace of the meditation throughout her body and called on the Light. A soft glow built quickly to brilliance. Allowing herself to sink into the Light, she grasped the crystal and felt the strong power pull her. She reached into it and felt it spread through her being.

"When you are filled with the light, I want you to think of pulling a protective bubble over you like a blanket or dome. Cover yourself completely. Concentrate on making it strong and impenetrable. Don't be distracted by anything from holding it in place. OK. Open your eyes but maintain your control and we will conduct an experiment.

When Amey opened her eyes, Jasper signaled. From out of the trees came a trio of masked men brandishing weapons. They rushed at Amey. Jasper continued to speak softly to her urging her to hold the protection in place and not be distracted. The masked men reached her quickly and Amey watched them stop dead in their track. She felt a pull on the protective barrier she projected and fought to hold it in place. When she looked over to Jasper, she saw a huge grin on his face. One of the masked men stepped back and pulled the covering over his head. Lirin emerged and grinned as much as Jasper. The final two men pulled off their masks to reveal her grandmother and Mother. Lirin was first to speak.

"Well done, Amey. Well done!"

Amey released the barrier and found herself hugged tight by an enthusiastic group. She felt drained by the experience but exhilarated as well.

"You did it, Amey. I knew you could but you were even better than I hoped. You're able to protect yourself and I'll show you how to extend that protection to others. I think you have just passed this part of the course," said Jasper. "I'm not saying that you know everything you need to know, but I'm satisfied you know enough for now. We'll do more tomorrow but we'll break for today."

"Oh, sweetheart, I'm so proud of you!" Rose had tears running down her face.

"Let's all go in and celebrate."

Grandmother Angeline put her arms around her daughter and granddaughter and walked them back to the Lodge. Lirin and Jasper followed behind.

"I wasn't sure about Jasper's plan but Lirin assured us you'd do just fine. I was so surprised to run into such a strong protective shield! You have indeed learned your lessons well. I know that we have a better chance at succeeding. Let's get Nanny Pearl to throw together another celebration for us all before we have to confront the Magician. We seem to be celebrating a lot in the last couple of days. Let's hope that continues."

Angeline led the jolly group into the kitchen and called out to Nanny Pearl to prepare another party.

Chapter Nine – Strategy

Amey's lessons continued daily but the more important business was to plan how to defeat the Magician. The family and a group of the leading men and women were meeting in secret in the town. Jasper outlined what they knew already.

"The Magician has attracted the corrupt and greedy to work for him. He has promised them wealth and power. What he can't win with bribes he controls with his mind. That is his greatest power. He has no compassion and will employ any means to get his way. What he wants is to destroy any opposition to him ruling both Altidio and Freo."

Angeline nodded in agreement. She knew Jasper had people out asking questions around the countryside.

"Do we know if he has brought weapons from his trip to the other world?"

"As far as we know he hasn't brought enough for his followers. He would need time to train his men how to use them and he knows we are not going to wait much longer to confront him. Don't underestimate the weapons that he does have, though. We don't think he has many in his force who have any powers. Personally, I don't think he trusts having any powers but his in control. His right-hand men do have some ability from what we've seen but nothing we can't overcome. They do have otherworld weapons. I saw them myself when they came to the farm. We will have to neutralize them quickly to prevent them using them against our people. It would be a slaughter"

Jasper looked around the table at the group assembled there. They were all ages and sexes. Some would do the fighting while others would coordinate the operation. His young apprentices would be under Lirin's direction.

"What we want to do is send groups of our more fully trained young men and women around the countryside to collect others with abilities into fighting groups. These groups can then organize the citizenry and instruct them in techniques to overcome the Magician's troops.

With any luck, we will be able to break his mind control over those in his employ but that isn't our priority. We need to convince the people that their greater numbers can overcome the might of the Magician's men. We will start in the city to support the rescue of Prince Alair."

Lirin took up the briefing.

"I will be leading the trainees. We have been setting up secure holding facilities. When we capture some of the men, they will be delivered to holding pens guarded by trained elders. Once we have depleted the Magician's forces seriously enough, we plan to pair our more advanced trainees with local forces to concentrate on the Magician's main force. His people are not brave, seasoned fighters but bullies and criminals. They have no loyalty to the Magician. When it looks like they will lose in the battle, they will probably cut their losses and run. We can't depend on that but think that is how it will go. We have observed this happening when they have met any serious opposition before."

Angeline considered the information that she was receiving. Her main concern was to distract the Magician so that Amey could rescue her father. She was sure that he wouldn't hesitate to kill Prince Alair out of spite if it looked like he was going to lose.

"While you are decoying the enemy's troops in the city, Rose, Amey and I will be working to release Prince Alair. Early in the morning on the day, we will secretly work our way close to the palace and then make our way in and wait for you to begin. Your tactics will create a diversion we hope will distract the Magician, giving us the time we need to find Alair. From what we have discovered about his state, we should have no problem with him. Rose and I will set up a guard while Amey attempts to break through the Magician's spell. I don't know how long this will take. We want to be a small, mobile group not weighed down with guards. We..."

Jasper interrupted saying,

"Milady, you are too important to risk without more security than that. We will handpick an escort for you. They will be familiar with the area and will not hinder your speed in any way. They will guard you from harm. This is something on which I insist! We know of people within the palace still loyal to Alair who will help you enter. After you get into the palace, they will hide you and we will post guards who will be able to warn you if the Magician arrives."

"Alright, Jasper, we will do it your way. I intend, however, to confront the Magician at some time. He needs to be removed from his position of influence so that we don't have his threat hanging over our heads."

Angeline met Jasper's eyes and a silent agreement was reached. He nodded his head and continued with the briefing.

"The enemy is armed with swords, bows and arrows, clubs and spears. Our citizens have some swords and spears and all have bow and arrow. They will use pitchforks and whatever else constitutes a weapon. They will be protected as much as possible during the battle by one of our trained men. It will be their responsibility to counteract any attempt by the enemy to control them.

The bulk of his men are massed near the capital. He wants to ensure that the city isn't captured. As has been said before, these are not seasoned fighting men but rather the worst sort of mercenary. Lirin, make sure that most of your best-trained men are in that area. I know you community leaders from those areas expect us to give you lots of backup. We will not disappoint you. Please organize your men so that we work together efficiently. The object is to lure and capture as many of the enemy as possible to keep them out of the major battle.

We will need to work fast. Get our men and women into place and assist the locals as much as possible. We'll break now but keep in touch. Secrecy is the key. Go back to your people and make as much preparations as you can. When we are ready, I will notify you immediately. Good day and Godspeed."

Everyone rose and said their goodbyes. They left singly and in pairs at intervals from the front and the back doors to attract as little attention as possible. Soon the room was clear. Angeline rose and thanked the owners for the use of the meeting room.

"Let's return to the Lodge. With things moving so swiftly toward the confrontation, we need to decide the best strategy for Amey. I don't think we need to leave all of it to her to decide. She needs to know what to do when she finds her father and how to free him."

The remaining group made their way back to the Lodge and gathered in the dining room at the refectory table. Angeline excused herself and left to retrieve the things they would need to formulate an effective strategy for Amey. When she returned, she was carrying a large, intricately embroidered bag in a rich purple velvet and the leather-bound book Rose took from the farmhouse. She placed the two items in the middle of the table and stood in front of them. All remained standing. She reached forward, undid the clasp fastening and opened the bag. She withdrew a purple velvet cloth done in a roll. Laying this on the table, she unrolled it to reveal within a collection of stones. They were a kaleidoscope of colour and variety of form. They winked and sparkled with inner life and were gemstones of exquisite beauty.

"What we have here are the 'Stones of Power.' Each one of these stones has a distinct character and usage. What we need to do now is create a healing ritual using the stones that will be most beneficial to Alair's situation. We don't know how much damage has been done or whether he is simply in a deep trance. I am hoping for the trance. That can possibly be reversed. We'll have to try anyway. We will include stones for every eventuality."

Angeline spread out the stones to separate them. Each was a thing of beauty. There were stones banded with rings of colour, blood red ones with deep lights, lavender ones to match Amey's eyes, blue ones of every shade and others that burst with all hues of the rainbow. She picked up one of intense black with a polished surface.

"This is obsidian- a protection stone. It can absorb negativity and would be helpful to reverse the Magician's spell. The ruby works in a similar way but also can repel the destructive forces wielded by him.

Then she chose a beautiful, lavender stone wrapped with alternating bands of white and darker purple.

"Banded amethyst cuts through illusion. With the boy Perrin, the Magician implanted a terrifying image to immobilize him - probably more out of maliciousness than for any other reason. This stone could help Alair and should be part of the healing ritual."

Jasper reached across the table and picked up a translucent stone the colour of seawater. He added it to the group of stones Angeline was creating.

"Aquamarine is a universal cleanser. It eases confusion. It should help if Prince Alair is in a trance or under some other mind control It also eases nerves."

Rose picked up a vivid blue stone with a glowing white star.

"Blue sapphire will also dispel confusion. We will need to convince him of the danger when we rescue him. He will need to be able to think clearly."

They continued in this way selecting the appropriate stones with beneficial powers for their mission. Some were to counteract the Magician's spell: others were to heal Alair. Amey picked one stone out and held it in front of her. It was the stone that matched her eyes- a clear lavender crystal that sparkled in her hand.

"This is my namesake stone. I've been taught amethyst is a healing stone that strengthens all healing energies. It is used to strengthen will power and mental clarity. It also protects travelers. I think we all need to carry one of these."

Everyone looked up at Amey with surprise.

"You don't need to look so surprised. You taught me about the powers of the stones years ago, Grandmother."

Amey was a little insulted by their reaction to her suggestion.

"You are right, Amey. I'm sorry. We were not including you in the process when you will have the most to do in the end. You have chosen well. Amethyst will protect us all." She selected another stone that blended the shade of Amey's stone with an orangish-yellow stone.

"Another stone has the same properties as amethyst but a second complimentary effect. Ametrine is both amethyst and citrine. Citrine can enhance your white light energy and help you to enter a deep state of meditation quickly. It is essential for you to be able to enter that state at will and, depending on the control used on your father, enhancing your energy should give you the power you need to reach him."

"Is there a different ritual for each thing you want to achieve or will a simple one do the same thing for all? I know there are rituals for all applications but are they really necessary?"

Jasper answered before her grandmother.

"Under circumstances where you have control, yes, there are specific rituals that work best. You will not be working under normal circumstances; time will be of the essence. We will teach you the appropriate ritual. However, because of the time constraint, you will also learn a simplified version of that ritual. But, yes, in answer to your question, if you are unable to use the appropriate ritual, a simple ritual prayer as you used before will work just as well."

"Your mother and I will be with you, Amey. We will help you in any way we can. What you need to concentrate on is learning the rituals and how to use the stones we choose here in the best way."

Angeline walked around the table and put her arm around Amey's shoulder.

"Try not to let yourself get weighed down with the responsibility that we've put on you. I know that's easy to say. Things will work out the way they were meant to work out. We can only do the best that we can and use the talents we were given to do good things. I have every confidence that you will do just fine. Now, let's get this organized so that Amey can feel some of that confidence herself. Rose, pass me the book, please."

Rose picked up the leather-bound book and passed it to her mother.

"This is the Book of Ritual, Amey. In it are all the prayers and instructions necessary for all the rituals we know. We would've used it to guide your instruction when you found out about your power but that option was taken from us."

Angeline opened it and began to leaf through the pages. Finding what she was looking for she put the book on the table.

"When we find where Prince Alair is in the palace, we will need some way to get him to lie down calmly. If what we have been told is accurate, that might not be too hard. However, we can't take that for granted. We will need to have some way to put him into a receptive state that will allow us to perform the ritual. There is a procedure in the book that will place him into a relaxed but still conscious state. It is called "Serenus Status" and places the person in a calm and serene state. The ritual uses a rose quartz to affect the state one wants to achieve. This is your namesake stone, Rose. In the ritual, the stone is held to the forehead. The ritual prayer reads,

'By your power through this stone
Peace and calm flow through me.
Fill the vessel giving rest
Leaving there serenity.'

That's one of the simpler ones. You know, it doesn't have to be Amey who does this part. Either Rose or I could and let Amey do the main healing of Alair's mind. What do you think, Amey?"

Amey was unsure what she should answer. Could she do it and perform the healing ceremony? She thought that the calming ritual sounded easy enough but it might be better to let either her grandmother or mother take that responsibility.

"It would be nice if you or mother could do it. Thank you."

"Good. Then, one or both of us will take this part of the procedure. Now, let's find the best ritual prayer for the hard part."

All of them listened as Angeline read out the different healing rituals and they weighed the merits of each one. There were many which dealt with trances or mind control but not exactly what they thought was needed. Finally, after much thought and discussion, they settled on one that seemed perfect for the occasion and not too hard for Amey to remember.

Amey read the instructions for the ritual that would accompany the healing prayer. She gathered the gemstones that they had chosen and began to lay them out according to the book. She visualized a body in front of her and started placing them in the order prescribed. It was hard to see what it would look like in her mind's eye. Lirin was watching her and noticed the frown.

"Why don't I let you practice on me? That way you can get a feel for how it will go. No need to go through the whole thing, though. I don't need you to free my mind."

He sat on the table and lay back making himself comfortable. Everyone laughed and Amey was a little embarrassed. Lirin opened one eye and asked,

"How do I look? Would you think I was in a trance?"

Amey couldn't think of anything smart to say so she just replied,

"If you're in a trance, don't you think you should be quiet? Well, seeing as you're willing, I might as well do a dry run."

She read the instructions again and looked at Lirin. She took his hands and turned them palm up at his sides. Choosing eight clear crystals, she laid them out in a cross shape on his chest putting the largest one closest to his heart. The gemstones that complimented the healing effect she placed in equal numbers on his palms. Finally, she lifted the beautiful banded amethyst and placed it in the center of his forehead.

Grandmother Angeline passed the ametrine gemstone to Amey.

"You should hold this in your hand with your crystal pendant to amplify your power."

Amey thanked her grandmother and held both stones in her right hand. Looking at the book she read to herself,

Through your healing Stones of Power
By my willing hand,
Open up the shuttered mind
Remove constraining bands.
Let your healing Light
Free the shackled mind,
Free the fettered spirit,
Leaving bonds behind.

Following instructions, Amey closed her eyes and tried the prayer from memory. She repeated it aloud word for word. She put her left hand as the Book directed on Lirin's head over the gemstone. Unexpectedly, she was engulfed in light and Lirin jumped. Amey pulled her hand back, Lirin sat up and they spoke at the same time.

"Wow!"

"Oh, Lirin, I'm sorry!"

"Good heavens, Amey. What happened? Are you alright, Lirin?"

Grandmother Angeline was worried and looked from her granddaughter to Lirin. The shocked look on both their faces turned to grins then to outright laughter. Lirin swung his legs over the edge of the table and placed his hand on Amey's shoulder. He spoke to the rest of the people around the table.

"Looks like Amey isn't going to have any trouble at all. Just by doing that run-through, she was able to send a powerful surge into me. It took me by surprise. I imagine it did her also."

Everyone was looking at Amey. She still had a smile on her face.

"Well, at least we know it works."

Chapter Eleven – Bear Claw Mountain

Amey awoke to a beautiful day. The sun was just rising and there were no clouds in the sky. When she went to the window and pushed it wide, the sound of birdsong filled the air. Her window gave her a view of her mountain with the mists swirling around the peak waiting for the rays of the sun to burn them off. She had been training nonstop for the last couple of days and, instead of feeling tired and drained, she felt exhilarated. There was so much to learn! Jasper started out with the basics but in the last couple of days he had turned to more in-depth study and training.

It was so important for Amey to feel confidence in her ability. From the first attempt at protecting herself from attack, she could now extend that protection to those around her. From moving a leaf around the table, Amey could cause the trees and bushes to stir and even lift smaller rocks and branches. She even felt that there was more in reserve when she did her exercises. She looked forward to every day and what new things that she could learn.

Her Mother was still asleep and Amey didn't want to disturb her. She quickly pulled on her clothes and quietly left their room to enter the bathroom down the hall. At least her grandmother and Jasper brought this improvement to their world! She brushed her teeth at the basin and made herself presentable before going downstairs to the kitchen.

Nanny Pearl was already up and preparing packed lunches. She had fruit and sandwiches made from her hearty brown bread wrapped in waxed cloth piled on the table ready to put in the two open packsacks on the chair.

"Good morning, Nanny Pearl. Isn't it a beautiful morning?"

She leaned in and gave Nanny a quick kiss on the cheek that had the old woman smiling broadly.

"It is indeed a lovely morning. Perfect for exploring nature, I think."

Amey looked at Nanny Pearl a little strangely. It was an odd response. She went over to the stove and saw there was already a pot of tea brewing. A plate of fresh muffins was cooling on a rack on the side table.

"Go on- get yourself a tea and a muffin. You can take them over to the table and I'll bring the rest of your breakfast. There's butter there already as well as milk and juice. Your grandmother will be down in a minute."

Nanny Pearl bustled over to the stove and stirred the pot of porridge. She took down three bowls and set them on a tray. Next came the sugar bowl, a jar of honey and a moisture-glazed jug of milk. There were bowls with raisins, dates and toasted walnuts to choose from to decorate the porridge. Amey heard footsteps on the stairs and turned a warm smile of greeting to her grandmother as she entered the kitchen.

"Good morning, Grandmother."

"Good morning, Amey, Nanny Pearl. Is your mother still sleeping?"

Her Grandmother followed the same route Amey just took and came to the table carrying her tea and took a muffin.

"Oh yes. I didn't want to wake her. You know she doesn't really like to get up this early anyway. Do you remember when I woke her early to tell her what a beautiful morning it was and she said it would be just as beautiful in a couple of hours and went back to sleep? She's definitely not a morning person!"

Angeline laughed as she sat down.

"No, no one can accuse her of that. She just doesn't know what she's missing."

"Doesn't care either, I'm thinking," said Nanny Pearl as she brought over the laden tray and set it on the table.

Noticing the three bowls, Amey said,

"Are you joining us this morning, Nanny?"

"No, my dear, I'm not. But I think this young man will be."

Amey looked to the door and in walked Lirin. He was dressed in his woodsman gear and set his equipment on the floor inside the door.

"Good morning, all. Lovely morning."

They exchanged 'good mornings' and Lirin went to get himself a tea. He brought it with him and joined them at the table as Nanny Pearl set out each of their bowls. He also took a muffin as the scent of them was too tempting. Silence ruled as everyone got down to the business of eating. They sat back satisfied after their hearty breakfast and finished their tea. Nanny brought over the teapot and refilled Angeline's cup.

"You two won't need a refill. I filled one of those fancy cups your grandmother brought here and you can take it with you. There's also containers of water that you can refill and enough food for the day."

Amey looked confused so her grandmother told her that Lirin had mentioned that she would love to go for a hike up Bear Claw Mountain if it could be arranged.

"I told him I thought it would do you good and we arranged it as a surprise for you this morning. You've worked so hard and I think a break is in order. Everything is ready and you have a beautiful day for it. What could be better? Just watch out for patrols."

Amey was ecstatic! Laughing, she hugged her grandmother and Nanny Pearl.

"What a wonderful surprise! This is just great!" and to Lirin, "Thank you for remembering."

"Let's get going. We don't want to waste the day."

Amey jumped up and looked to see what she had on, thankful that it would do for the hike and she wouldn't have to go change. Lirin was filling the packs while Amey went to find her jacket. When she put on her pack, she knew that Lirin had taken the heavier one. She wouldn't complain because she knew he would be embarrassed but determined to even it out at some time along the way.

They headed out on the forest path that led directly to the mountain. Amey looked up to see, as she expected, the sun warming the top burning off the morning mists. She was amazed how similar the two places were. She couldn't have told the difference if asked. As it was early in the spring, when they followed the path into the woods, Amey could see clearly in all directions because the understory was wide open. The ferns were just showing their distinctive fiddleheads and the young trees and bushes were cloaked in various shades of tiny, soft green leaves. Amey could see that the same salmonberry and thimbleberry bushes were here also. The new growth on the mosses underfoot were the prettiest shade of lime green. Later in the year, all the trees would be densely covered in lush foliage and the ferns would be more than waist high blocking the view.

Lirin set a leisurely but steady pace. The path was too narrow to walk abreast so they continued single file. The quiet allowed Amey to let her mind wander.

"Lirin, have you been to the farm?"

"Yes, I have, a couple of times, but it was a few years ago. Jasper brought me there to show me some of your world. You were away at school and your mother and grandmother were off somewhere also. I was amazed by the advancements that had been made there over what one finds here."

"Do you know if the mountain here is exactly the same as the one there? I mean, is it made up of the same rock, does it have a cave like the one there? I find it hard to think that the same mountain could be there and here also."

"Jasper and I used to explore this mountain often. He said that it was so similar that it would be hard to tell apart. We would go hunting gemstones here or just go on camping trips to relax."

"That's what grandmother and I used to do! I had planned this school break to climb and explore. I spend most of my holidays from school on Bear Claw Mt."

"Jasper uses that name. I guess I got used to it because that's how I think of it, too."

"Before we came here, Jasper and I went up the mountain to a cave where Grandmother and I would shelter on our trips. That's where he told me about my family and the gemstones. Do you think we could go up there so I can see how similar they are?"

"Sure, we can. It would be a good spot to stop for lunch."

They were in among the tall cedars and spruce and, as they passed by, squirrels chittered a warning at them from the trees. The fallen logs that littered the ground were covered in moss and you could see the new ferns and seedling trees sprouting all around them. The morning sun wasn't high enough yet to pierce the canopy but cast a green glow over everything. The air was fresh with a slight chill but the walking warmed them quickly though they were keeping to a relaxed pace. They weren't in any hurry today.

Lirin led the way along a clearly visible path that wound through the stately timber. Amey saw that other paths broke away from this one going in every direction. Some of those went deeper into the woods while others headed toward the base of the mountain. They were approaching the mountain in an area where there was a slide on the mountain at the farm and she found it looked much the same here. Turning away from the mountain to skirt the foot of the slide, they cut back through the boulder-strewn forest to reach the path to the cave. Newly fallen rocks showed up starkly against the moss and lichen covered ones that had been there from previous slides. In the spring, it wasn't safe to climb over the rocks in the slide path. You had to be prepared for one at any time. You couldn't outrun it over the uneven footing on the rockfall.

They reached the foot of the mountain and took a break to finish the tea while it was still hot. They sat on fallen logs leaning back against the jumbled rocks while they enjoyed the fragrant tea.

"Do you know why my grandmother hasn't brought back any of the technology from my world? I would think it could make everyone's life easier. I was grateful that they put in bathroom facilities at least."

"What I know of the world where you were raised, I'm not sure that all that technology is an improvement. Sure, you have electricity to power lights and machines but what about the rivers where they put the dams or the pollution from the ones who burn coal to make the power. The land has been stripped of all its riches and little has been put back. What about all the weapons that have been made as an improvement over what came before. Now people can kill each other faster and in bigger numbers. Jasper showed me all these things when I was there after I asked him why we didn't have them also. He pointed out that all the advancements came too quickly before anyone knew the consequences. He told me that it was better to introduce improvements slowly after you weighed all the possible problems that could be caused by what you do. We can look to your world and see what to avoid. I think I agree but it would be great to have some of the things that I saw, especially if there were none of the problems that came with them. I especially love computers!"

Amey smiled at the enthusiasm of his last comment. She had thoughts about the damage progress and technology had done to her world also but not when she had asked the question. It was true that mankind had done serious damage, some irreparable, to earth. Perhaps waiting had been for the best.

She enjoyed talking to Lirin. It was good to have someone who could relate to her and who she could bounce her thoughts off and who could make her ask questions of herself.

"Well, you can study all the things that would be good to have and see where we made the mistakes. That way you could have all the good stuff without the bad."

It was a lovely thought but Amey knew that her grandmother and Jasper had done the right thing in not making wholesale changes. She smiled ruefully at Lirin who then stood up reaching out to pull her to her feet.

"Let's go. We can get the hard part of the hike done before the sun gets too high. It looks like it's going to be a warm day."

Lirin went to hoist his pack but Amey reached it first and added some of the things in his to hers. At Lirin's look of surprise, Amey said,

"I can carry more than you think, Lirin. Thank you for the thought, but it isn't necessary. Grandmother and I used to come back from a hike with more weight in our packs than we went out with fully loaded. We'd have them so full of rocks that I'm surprised they didn't split."

Once she had rearranged them to her liking, she pulled hers on and gave the other to Lirin. He just shook his head and pulled it in place on his back. He laughed and said over his shoulder,

"Suit yourself but I don't want to hear any complaints about it later. Nor will I carry it for you even if you beg."

Amey chuckled and said, "Fat chance of that happening. Let's go."

Lirin went first. He wound his way through the rocks, keeping to the faint path. They climbed up steadily. Looking to the left, you could see where snow had slid down not too long ago. It mounded over the rocks and dripped between to form rivulets that ran together into larger ones. This was why it was so unstable here in the spring. The water undermined the rocks as it flowed down and around the stones. The sun was higher now and would contribute to the melt. You could hear running water everywhere on the mountain. New waterfalls would appear in spring only to disappear completely in summer. Hiking at that time meant you had to know where to find the water or bring lots with you. That wouldn't be a problem now.

When they came out above the canopy of the forest, they paused to look out over the tops of the trees at the valley below. You could see smoke rising from the morning fires dotting the landscape. Lirin pointed out where various communities were situated.

"Which direction is the capital? How far away is it?"

Lirin located the place to direct Amey's eyes and said,

"Do you see where the trees give way to a cleared area? That is where the road is that leads to the city. If you follow that clearing to the right, the road will run straight for about 10 miles directly to the capital. You can't see it from here because of this knoll that juts into the valley."

"Is there a harbour there? If we were on the mountain at the farm, the direction you indicate leads to the town of Grenian which has an active harbour. That's where I first saw the Magician's men getting off a huge yacht."

"Yes, there is. It is used most of the year by fishing boats. We sometimes get the trading ships also but we don't export anymore since the Magician took over. He cheated too many people and they just quit dealing with us. It has meant that our industry has almost ground to a standstill but still he demands payment. Our people are stretched thin trying to support their families," Lirin said bitterly.

He looked away from the valley and turned to the path again. They continued to climb. The sun was shining fully on the rock face across the slide and could be felt reflecting back at them. Just as they were about to round an outcropping, they felt the ground quiver. Lirin pushed Amey back around the rock and they hurried farther away from the edge of the slide. A rumbling growl started softly and grew continually until it was a roar. The ground shook violently and they held on to the cliffside. First came a small quantity of loose rock and then the bulk of the slide raced by. The noise was tremendous – more of a concussion that could be felt reverberating in their chests. Clouds of dust boiled up over the lip of the slide zone and Lirin and Amey hastily pulled their hood over their heads covering their faces. As quickly as it began, it ended. The breeze generated by the passing rock swirled the dust away. They waited a while longer before they looked out from under their hoods. Things looked pretty much the same as they had before the slide except for the addition of newly fallen boulders. Lirin eased away from their shelter, walked over to the edge and looked down. He listened carefully and even knelt to put his ear to the ground.

"I can't hear any vibrations. That could be it. What do you want to do- go ahead or turn around and go back?"

Amey too was listening keenly. She had been on the mountain before during a slide but this had been much closer. It had shaken her but she wanted to continue the hike. She wasn't sure when she would have another chance.

"Let's go on, OK? At least as far as the cave. If the path is covered, we might not have any choice in the matter."

"Come on but stick close to me."

They made their way around the outcropping, pushing aside small boulders as they went. The cave wasn't much farther and they could see that the path wasn't damaged. They still continued with an ear cocked for the slightest sound of another slide. One more turn and they would be there.

When they went around the last rock before the cave, the scene that met them was fantastic. The path usually led beyond the cave mouth but was now blocked with a pile of broken rock. Some had tumbled into the cave, partially blocking the entrance. They walked to the edge of the rocks and tried to see over the top but couldn't quite make it. They certainly weren't about to climb on the pile to see. It wouldn't take much to start it all moving.

"Well, I guess we end here." Lirin looked up to gauge the time. "We might as well have our lunch break and rest a bit. Let's go into the cave so that we aren't exposed out here. If you feel any rumble or shaking, get out of the cave and run back down the path."

He lowered his pack to the ground and pushed aside a few rocks to clear a way for easy departure. Amey found two good size stone and set them where they could use them as seats. They worked together pulling out sandwiches and fruit. They each had water bottles. When everything was assembled, they sat on their rocks and stretched out their legs. The cave was cool and felt good on their heated skin. Soon the sun would round the knoll and shine onto the path and entrance. Amey looked over at Lirin and laughed.

"You should see your face. It's covered in the dust. Is mine?"

"Sure is." They both pulled out a rag, spilled some of their water onto the cloth and scrubbed the dirt off their faces using it also to wipe their hands and dust each other off. Feeling cleaner, they opened their sandwiches, not surprised to find they were very hungry. They ate in silence watching the sun on the mountainside opposite them.

Amey looked around the cave to see how much it resembled the one in her world. There wasn't any difference to see. There was even a pile of wood against the wall. Lirin saw the direction of her gaze and said,

"Jasper always makes sure that there is a wood supply here for any time we or anyone else need to stay."

"It's the same in my world. The only thing not the same is the cooking sticks. We have them there but none are here."

"Yes, there are, but I see some rocks have fallen over them. Looks like some loose stone from the wall fell in during the slide."

The thought that the cave itself might not be secure made them a little uneasy. They looked back at the entrance of the cave just in time to see the sun burst onto the rocks at the door. The light flashed on something in the rock pile. Both Lirin and Amey got up and walked over to see what it could be. To their surprise, nestled among the broken rock, were a number of stones which had crystals in them. They gingerly lifted them out of the pile and set them on the ground behind them while they searched for more. They were amazed how many they found. Amey moved aside a fairly large stone and gasped in awe. Lying there was a magnificent faceted crystal the size of the palm of her hand. It was beautiful!

Amey held it up and the sunlight fractured on its surface. She turned to Lirin holding the crystal in both hands. She couldn't say anything. Lirin reached out his hand and lightly touched the surface. He, too, was in awe.

"Wow, Amey. That is amazing! I've never seen a more beautiful one before."

Lirin continued to look for more but couldn't find any. He collected the ones they'd already found, pulled out his extra shirt and wrapped up the crystals. Amey went to her pack and pulled out a T-shirt. She used this to wrap up her fabulous stone and carefully placed it among the rest of the contents of her pack. Lirin put the others in his and they silently agreed to end their trip. They wanted to get back to the Lodge and show off their find.

Amey looked around and thought of the gift just given to her by her mountain.

"I think Bear Claw Mountain wants to help us. Look at the powerful tool it has just given to us. I will use it in the ritual to rescue my father."

Lirin nodded in agreement at the fanciful thought of a gift from the mountain. They prepared to leave the cave. They removed their jackets for the sun would be too warm with them on.

Amey stopped as she left, turned to look at her mountain and said a quiet 'Thank you.' The trip down was a lot hotter with the sun beating down on the rock. It went quicker than the trip up and they reached the bottom in short order. Just stepping back under the trees brought cool relief. The walk in the cooler shade was a relief. They soon heard flowing water. They had emptied their water bottles and stopped at the swiftly flowing stream to refill them.

"Lirin, would you mind if I cleanse and my charge new crystal in this stream? I can't wait until we get back and this is a perfect opportunity. I want to remove any negative energy held in the stone so it is ready to help me train."

Lirin agreed and Amey took her wonderful crystal from the folds of her shirt. She knelt on the edge of the stream and, holding the crystal in the cage of her fingers, lowered it into the cold, crisp flowing water. She held it there for a few minutes until her hands were too cold to continue and then laid it on a rock in the sunlight while she warmed her hands under her arms. Once she had some feeling in them, she picked up her crystal, closed her eyes and linked to the stone. She spoke her instruction in her mind and charged the crystal to protect and enhance the power of the user. The ritual didn't take long and Amey separated her thoughts from the crystal. She put it in her jacket pocket because she couldn't resist the chance to feel the smooth surface under her hand.

They rested a little while longer before continuing back to the Lodge. They went carefully, keeping alert for any sign of patrols. They had just turned away from the mountain when they heard a twig snap. Lirin pulled Amey close and stepped in the shelter of a large cedar. Amey reached into her pocket and clutched the crystal. She felt the strong pull of the stone. She also noticed something else. Leaning close to Lirin's ear, she whispered,

"There's no birdsong."

She knew it was the Magician's men. Soon they could hear whispered voices.

"I heard something moving over this way. Come on."

There were three of them and they were coming directly toward them! Amey took her crystal and held it in both hands. She needed to distract them. She closed her eyes and reached for the power in the crystal. It was very strong and her inner being was quickly engulfed in a bright white Light. She sent out her thoughts and sought something that she could use. In her mind, she could see the men. She could also feel the silent birds and animals around her. Perhaps she could startle one of them so that it would move and draw the three men. Because Lirin held her, he was aware what she was doing. It was as if they were one in the effort. He directed her inner gaze to the pair of deer who stood quietly watching the men. Amey was surprised to find Lirin taking part in her attempt but welcomed his suggestion. She reached out to the deer and touched their minds. She sent the warning, 'Flee, flee' and felt their reaction. It was as if they had felt her hand. They were frightened and bolted from cover, almost knocking down the three men in their haste to escape. Before they could react, the deer were gone from sight.

"There's your 'something moving,'" said the one man in disgust. 'You're beginning to see rebels behind every tree!"

"They probably are behind every tree."

The man who'd heard the sound was eager to get back to the open road. He wasn't happy to be in the woods. He was always afraid that the rebels would attack on their turf. He passed close by them walking swiftly to get back to the open air.

Lirin and Amey stayed still until there was no sound. Lirin grinned at her and said with a gleam in his eyes,

"That was fun! What a rush!"

Amey was less inclined to see it as fun but Lirin's mood was infectious.

"I can't say I was having fun. I was scared to death! But it was kind of fun, I guess."

She too was grinning.

"Let's not waste any time and get out of here before we run into anyone else."

They carefully left their hiding place. Amey was excited and wanted to show off her new crystal. Lirin couldn't wait to tell everyone about their experience and how Amey reacted in the face of danger. He took Amey's hand and together they hurried back to the Lodge.

Chapter Twelve - Campaign

The next few days were spent in preparation. Information came in from various districts but the most important news came from the capitol. It was imperative that they knew the setup in the city. They had to know the Magician's strength and the location of his men so that they could safely plan for the rescue party. It was clear that the Magician was still actively looking for their location as they learned that more and more people were being interrogated and imprisoned. Groups of his men were going around the countryside harassing the citizens even beating those they thought might have any knowledge of their stronghold. How many men were left in the capitol was vital data that would determine how they went forward.

Jasper met with the team leaders and ran through the plans with them step by step. He wasn't leaving anything to chance. The group was made up of seasoned practitioners as well as talented and well-trained young men and women. These people would be with the citizenry in the coming confrontation that they knew would come once they rescued the prince. Jasper made sure that their abilities were honed to near perfection. Their talents were varied. Some were healers and would be used to reverse the Magician's effects on his fighters. Some were adept at protection and would guard the townspeople. The ones who had the most control over the stones were given special assignments. They were preparing the whole country to be ready. The people were not fighters but would join with other to oust the Magician in support of their queen and Prince Alair. Jasper took special care picking the forces that would be around the palace. He wanted to have powerful forces there to protect the Queen, Rose and Amey.

Lirin was away often. Jasper had come to rely on his quick mind and abilities. His focus was on the people in his age group. He had traveled the countryside organizing other young trainees who had been assigned different bases of operation. He instructed them to work closely with the citizens as he did. In each group was one young person who showed exceptional talent. They were there to use their superior skills in case of unforeseen events. The young adults were enthusiastic in their desire to fight back against the tyranny that had been their life. They saw the effects on their parents and knew the stories of how it used to be and they wanted that for themselves and their families. Lirin had to temper that enthusiasm with caution because the Magician was a formidable foe. They had to be disciplined and controlled to have a chance to win the day. Lirin searched out any among these young people whose potential was untapped and tested them to see what powers needed to be developed. When he found anyone who showed promise, he directed them to the teachers so that they could be trained and their abilities directed.

Amey continued to study and practice. She explored the range of her talent, tried different things and other ways to approach a task. Things she had never even dreamed of were now possible and came easier to her with every passing day. With the Book of Ritual, she was able to learn specific prayers and the steps required to complete each one. Her Grandmother advised that she concentrate on those that would be needed in the coming rescue and confrontation. She studied closely the properties of each gemstone and marked those offering the most protection.

She spent her spare time exploring the Lodge. It was an amazing structure built from massive polished timbers and ceilings that soared to rough-hewn beams. Upon entering the main gathering room, light from the windows kindled a glowing flame in the depth of the wood which was mostly cedar but was highlighted with accents of paler birch, alder and, what Amey was told, was cottonwood that appeared almost white. Care had been taken that each element blended with the whole. Wide-planked floors were polished to a high sheen that further enhanced the light and the fire in the massive stone fireplace added a cheery warmth. The walls held an array of decorative art from detailed pen and ink drawings of landscapes and figure studies of animals and birds to oil paintings and watercolours which hung side by side with polished pieces of fanciful wood sculptures. They all blended to add character to the room. The handmade hooked rugs brightened the floors in a creative collection of colours and decorative quilts and knitted afghans were draped over chair and sofas. Even the furnishings were made with style and grace as well as strength to stand up to the demands of the many inhabitants. Gracefully wrought stairs with polished handrails wound their way up to the upper floors.

There were many rooms used for the student activities- everything from basic classrooms any student would recognize to rooms for exercise, relaxing and a special one for craftsmen to ply their trades. It was here that Amey found the jewelry making supplies and tools. Making jewelry had been taught at school last year and Amey had fashioned gifts for her mother and grandmother. Thinking how perfect this was, she chose some fine silver wire, clasps and tools. There was no one about, so, Amey put her supplies on one of the worktables and went back to her room to collect the rest of the things she would need. She had a few hours to spare and thought that she would make protection amulets for her family, Jasper and Lirin. She picked up fine pointed pliers, a small-headed hammer and several different files. At school she was able to use a soldering iron or strong industrial glues but they weren't available here. She had chosen the stones with care, had cleansed and charged them and now carefully caged them in silver wire. Using her hammer, she bent, twisted and fused the join into a ring then hammered it flat When she had prepared each stone, she chose the ones that would work best together and clustered them lining up the loops at the end to attach together. She took meticulous care with each stone to be sure that they were secure and then linked each stone into the amulet. The final loop was formed to attach to the cord. Each person would have those stones suited best to their powers and all included a sparkling, clear crystal and, due to her recent experience, an ametrine.

Amey worked with skill and speed and soon had five distinctive amulets spread out before her on the table. Not only would they protect those who wore them but they looked good also. She threaded her pieces onto the braided cords she'd found and securely attached the clasps. Leaning back, she surveyed her work with satisfaction. These protection amulets were all she could offer to those close to her. She hoped they would be enough to see them all safe. Putting everything back in its proper place, she took her pieces and brought them to her room.

The next day, Amey and her grandmother were sitting together on the porch having tea after the morning lessons. Angeline was looking through the reports that Jasper had given to her that morning. Amey had always been a good student. She was fascinated with her newfound power and eagerly practiced the chants, prayers, and rituals that accompanied each application.

"Grandmother, can you do all these rituals?"

Angeline answered absently,

"I'm not sure that I have needed to do all of them but, the ones that I used worked well."

"The Book gives all the prayers and rituals but doesn't say what we can or can't do? I mean, what are the limits of the power?"

Angeline stopped what she was doing and considered the question.

"I don't know that anyone has actually figured out the limits. I've never experimented with the possibilities. We've only used the powers that we needed to meet a certain need. Before, we lived a peaceful life and, I guess, we weren't challenged the way you are today. We used what we needed. We'll have to ask Jasper if he knows."

"Ask me what?"

Jasper came around the corner. He helped himself to tea and one of the cakes Nanny Pearl had delivered at the end of the lesson. He took a seat opposite them at the table.

"Amey was just asking what the limits are of what we can do with the stones."

Jasper considered the question with care. It was something he'd considered before but hadn't explored. It was probably more important now and hadn't been done.

"I'm not sure that it's written anywhere what can be done with the power stones. They hold in their essence that energy obtained from the earth and ultimately from God. We are restricted only by our strength and control. I suppose anything is possible. I haven't explored this myself."

Amey considered this and wondered aloud,

"Do you suppose that the stones might just be something physical for us to concentrate on and not really necessary to accomplish the task? Like a statue we say prayers in front of. I mean, it seems unlikely that God would need to use stones, don't you think?"

Jasper and Angeline looked surprised and exchanged quick glances. They didn't seem to know what to say.

Jasper answered first.

"The stones have always been used. They are the only way that we know to control and focus the power and the ritual is an important part of it. What you are suggesting is out of the realm of our knowledge and not something that has been considered. What has brought about your questions?"

"I don't know. It just didn't seem that God would need to use a stone to empower someone he wanted to do His will. It was just a question that occurred to me."

Grandmother Angeline went to sit beside Amey and put her arm over her shoulder. She looked at her granddaughter and smiled.

"You know, Amey, you amaze me sometimes. I have never even considered such a thing being possible in all my life. Here you are, newly informed of your power, and you are already exploring beyond the accepted norms. I wish we had answers for your questions, but, be assured we will try to find them."

"Thank you, Grandmother."

Amey went back to practicing her lessons while Jasper and Angeline sat back drinking their tea and pondering her questions. In all likelihood, Amey would be the one to explore just how far one could go and they looked forward to where she would lead them all.

The day chosen to launch their offensive was grey and cool. It looked as if the rain would come soon. Amey gave each person the jewelry she had made for them.

"I made a special protection amulet for each one of you. I hope that it helps protect you from danger and can keep you safe."

She put the amulets over their heads and watched them pick them up to look at from where they lay on their chests. Jasper hugged her and Lirin said a quiet 'thank you.' Her mother and grandmother both kissed her and exclaimed over the workmanship. Grandmother Angeline pulled her into her arms and said as she stoked her hair,

"These are powerful stones of protection you have assembled for us, Amey. If anything will keep us safe, these will. Thank you."

Jasper escorted Angeline, Rose, and Amey into the city in the early hours before dawn to escape notice. He left them in the care of Lirin while he went off to oversee the preparations. Lirin would stay with them until the time when they would go with the scullery maids, cleaners and cook who would see them safely into the palace. These household staff lived in the city and went to the palace every morning to work. They were loyal to Alair and wanted to help in any way that they could. The weather worked in their favour.

Amey got her first glimpse of the palace. She wasn't sure what she had expected but a vision of a turreted building with tall steeples out of fairy tales had flashed through her mind. What she saw instead was a massive 3-story structure build of a light grey stone with arched windows outlined in white. Around the top of the building was a parapet with evenly spaced openings. The corners of the structure had alternating grey and white stones marching up to the roof and around the impressive carved double doors. The building could've looked cold and forbidding but there was instead a lightness to it remaining despite the ravages done to it by the current inhabitants. Some of the elegant stone urn planters were toppled while others were filled with dead stems of long-forgotten plants. No care had been taken to remove the detritus that built up around the base of the building and bordering the stair leading to the entrance. The façade with the curtainless window gave off an air of sadness.

The family would go in the side service entrance dressed as kitchen help covered in cloaks to protect them from the chill. The palace workers would hide them until it was safe to go search for Alair. Two guards were dressed as cleaners and would ensure the safety of the Queen, Rose, and Amey. Lirin left them with the kitchen staff when they arrived. Wishing them 'Godspeed,' he melted back into the mists to join with Jasper and the others waiting to start the offensive.

Walking in the deepening cold mist, they drew their cloaks tightly around their bodies and pulled their hoods close over their faces. Not two blocks from the palace, their group encountered a patrol of the Magician's men. They were on their rounds grumbling about having to be out in the miserable weather. They were not inclined to give their group more than a cursory inspection.

"What are you people up to this early in the morning?" asked the leader. His men didn't make any effort to search the group nor did the leader demand it. The cook stepped forward and threw back his hood challenging him.

"What do you think we're doing? We're going to work at the palace as usual. We go there every day. You see us every day. Why are you stopping us?"

"We have orders to question everyone. There's rumours flying around the city about so-called loyalists and the like. We're just doing our job. Lord knows we'd rather be somewhere else in this weather. Go on, now. Get on your way."

The patrol gave them no more notice and hurried on their way back to their quarters to warm themselves around the fire and drink their coffee laced, even at this early hour, with the rum that they smelled on their breath. The cook pulled his hood back up, turned to the group behind him, and blew out his breath in a sigh of relief.

"That was close! If these guys weren't so lazy, we could've been in trouble. Let's hurry now in case there are more. Looks like there's something in the wind."

He turned and hurried the group on their way. They reached the palace in a short time and entered through the kitchen door. They found themselves in a vast room that, even at this early hour, was warm from the fire in the enormous woodstove. The live-in staff would've been down to start the stove before they went to the rest of the palace to lay fires in all the occupied rooms. The staff removed their cloaks and hung them up on hooks in the cavernous pantry off to the right of the kitchen. In the short time she had lived there, Rose had never been in the kitchen nor had she known any of the staff except those she'd dealt with upstairs. She looked around with great interest. The cook led the family to the back of the pantry where another door opened onto stairs. These stairs led up into the whole palace. The serving and cleaning staff used them to get to every part of the building. They were offered stools to sit on behind the door while they waited. It would be awhile before the palace rose and went about their business. Here they would wait until they received word that the battle was joined in the city. Their two guards dressed as cleaners went out to carry buckets and brooms and scout out the palace in the hopes of finding where Prince Alair was held. The staff weren't allowed to serve him directly so they weren't sure where he could be found. Angeline, Rose, and Amey settled on their seats, leaned back against the wall and waited. All they could do now was wait.

Dawn was breaking. In the city, Jasper was keeping to the shadows to escape the notice of the patrols. He was heading to the last post he wanted to inspect before the battle began. Here was where he would fight. It seemed the Magician was hearing rumours and getting nervous. Jasper found the citizenry ready in all the places he'd visited so far. There was a determined anger in those he met and he hoped they could keep it in check. He knew it would be hard. The ordinary person in the city had suffered more than those in the country. The Magician demanded their food and money and his men were a brutal sort who didn't mind breaking a few heads in the process. The women didn't dare go out alone. Even the children with their carefree enjoyment of life knew to keep quiet and out of sight when they saw the roving bands of mercenaries. The jails were full of citizens arrested on trumped up charges and left there with little to eat. Were it not for their families smuggling in provisions, they might well have died there. They didn't go before a judge and, if the family wanted to get them out, they had to find the money to buy their release.

Their plan for the diversion was simple really. Lirin would enter the main square with an armed group of young men within full view of the palace. They would make enough noise to attract attention. They hoped this would draw out a force to meet the supposed threat. While the palace guards were distracted by the action happening out front, men and women would try to gain access to the jails and release all the prisoners. They had been warned ahead of time by their families when they delivered food what was being planned and to be ready if an escape could be orchestrated. Everyone knew what would happen to them if the Magician turned his anger on those left behind. Lookouts were posted while the rest went in. They overpowered the turnkey and hurriedly opened all the cells. Those who needed assistance were supported. They would not exit into the streets but turn aside once out the door and head around to the back of the palace and make their way to the woods in behind where carts and wagons would be waiting and they would be whisked away to safety and care.

Hidden in buildings in the side streets and alleyways, reinforcements would attack the Magician's men as they chased the troublemakers and, hopefully, overpower the force. They'd be taken away to the holding pen set up outside the city. This tactic would be repeated as long as it worked. They would then have to bring in their fighting force.

Jasper reached the shuttered building and tapped a signal on the door. He could hear the sound of muffled voices and the door opened a crack. When he was recognized, the door was quickly opened wide enough for him to enter. The room was filled with men and women carrying every sort of weapon. They were all dressed in dark clothes with hoods to pull up for when they went out. They were a grim lot. He asked quietly,

"Are you all ready?"

He received a unanimous murmured reply. One tall, burly man Jasper recognized as the blacksmith spoke for the group.

"Aye, we're ready to get rid of those filthy beggars. There's not a man or woman here who can wait to get our city back. You just tell us when and we'll follow."

"I've been to all the gathering places and this is my last. We won't have to wait long. We have a diversion planned that will draw out the guards and the Magician's forces to chase after the men running from the square. They will be splitting up to run down different roads so they are let past where there are people are stationed. I will fight with you. Wait 'til you hear the commotion outside. You know the plan. Take down as many as you can and we have people to take them away."

Jasper reached up to touch the amulet under his shirt and felt the comfort of it. He placed a lot of confidence in the piece Amey made and charged. He knew her power and couldn't have asked for better protection. Not that he expected it to do all the work. The saying, 'The Lord helps those who help themselves' were words he lived by. He leaned back against the wall and waited.

Several streets away, Lirin and a group of young men gathered just outside of the main square in sight of the palace. When everything was in place, they noisily entered the square and the guards on the palace wall were seen to hurry away to spread the alarm. Lirin pressed his hand over Amey's amulet and sought the power that resided there. Posted in various buildings in side streets in front of them were other groups of men and women. They would wait until the Magician's guards and mercenaries engaged the decoy force and chase them passed their doors. Once the battle was joined, they would rush in and try to overwhelm them. Lirin spoke quietly and confidently to his people.

"We are fighting evil here today. I will protect you as much as I can but do not expect any mercy from these men. Fight for your city and your country. May God protect us all."

Down the street from the palace came the Magician's forces. There were about thirty or forty seasoned fighters. They didn't wear uniforms but carried similar weapons. They were cruel looking men and a formidable enemy who expected to make short work of these young loyalists. Lirin could see archers on the wall and hoped the gifted gemstone novices would be able to project strong enough shields to deflect the worst of the injury from flying shafts. The guards were assuming the loyalists sought to take the palace. Their main objective, however, was to remove as many men as possible from the battle.

His men hoisted their weapons in preparation. They waited for the attackers to get in closer. The mercenaries expected them to run in front of their superior manpower. When they held their ground, they saw surprise in the enemy's eyes but still they came, taunting them to run home to mama. Lirin had picked the strongest to be in the vanguard. Lirin had cast a protective shield around his people and held it in place against the attack. When the mercenaries closed the distance and charged, his men fought them fiercely and then dispersed to run down the side streets out of view of the palace. The enemy showed their frustration and increased the level of violence and followed. Just when Lirin felt the greatest strain on his protective powers, the side streets erupted with men and women who fell on the mercenaries from behind and brought them down with clubs and sheer numbers. They hurried to secure their hands and feet and passed them off to those who came forward with carts to haul them off. The battle was fierce but short-lived. Their plan had worked beautifully.

Lirin knew that the same scene was being repeated in other streets around the palace. He could hear the yelling and sounds of battle. He sought out the injured among his people. He healed those that he could and eased the pain of those who needed more care. There weren't many injuries. He was happy to see that his group had fared quite well. With those who were still able to fight, they hurried toward the nearest sounds of battle to lend their aid.

Jasper could hear the battle start and went to the door. There were the cries of the wounded mingling with the angry shouts of the citizens. This post was situated on one of the direct routes from the palace to the square. Across the road, he could see other doors opening tentatively to scan the street. They were expecting reinforcements from the palace to hurry down this way to come on the battle from the side and overpower the rebel group.

Jasper closed the door until all that was left was a crack to look through. He motioned for his people to get ready. Here they came! Hurrying down the road in no particular formation came a large troop of men. Their leader was yelling at them to "Move it" and the men were spread out without thought of defense. When they entered the zone between the buildings filled with loyalists, they were surprised to find themselves under attack from angry citizens who fell on them with determination. They poured out of the buildings on either side of the street. They were hit with clubs and battered down, finally falling under the surprisingly powerful assault. Just as in the main square, carts and wagons were drawn into the street and the Magician's men were loaded on and hauled away. Jasper helped heal the ones who were injured and was glad that their ambush had worked as planned. Surprise had worked in their favour but Jasper knew that the enemy wouldn't fall for it again. He led his men toward the sound of battle. He hoped that they had diverted the Magician's attention enough to help Angeline, Rose, and Amey rescue Alair.

Chapter 13- Rescue

The sound of the battle penetrated the palace walls. Their guards had returned having discovered what they thought was the room where Alair was being held. Angeline questioned them closely.

"Did you see anyone go in or out?"

"No, milady, but one of the palace workers had been ordered to lay a fire in the room this morning. He saw no one when he was in the room but thought there might have been someone moving in the adjoining one."

"Thank, you. You can lead us back to this room?"

"Yes, milady. We need to wait awhile, though. The Magician is still in his rooms. You need to wait until he goes to his office or the garrison to see what is happening."

Just then, one of the serving staff hurried into the kitchen.

"There's fighting in the city! I saw troops leaving the palace to fight with the loyalists. There was a group of them in the square but I couldn't see how many. I was serving the Magician's breakfast and he just pushed me aside and hurried from the room."

The cook pulled her over to a stool and sat her down.

"You're sure the Magician is gone from his rooms?"

"Oh, yes, I'm sure. He called to his guards and they ran down the stairs with him."

The cook looked over to Rose, his Prince's wife.

"Milady, this sounds as good a time as any. We will alert the rest of the staff who are loyal to keep a lookout and warn you if the Magician is seen returning. We will help in any way that we can and keep an eye on those who are not for the prince."

"Thank you. What is your name?"

"Oscar, milady," and he doffed his cook's hat in a sweeping bow.

"Thank you then, Oscar."

Angeline addressed Oscar and the rest of the kitchen staff who stood by.

" I don't know how long we will be, but we will return this way to make our escape. Look for us to come through here in a hurry."

She turned and motioned the rest of her group to follow her. She directed the two guards to lead and they cautiously made their way up the staircase. The further they entered the main part of the palace, the louder the sounds of battle became. The halls were empty. When they passed one of the many windows facing the town square, they could see men fighting in the distance but didn't stop to watch. Amey fingered her amulet and prayed for the safety of those leading the loyalists.

It had been a long time since Rose had been in this palace and she was surprised how little things had changed. It saddened her to notice signs of neglect but saw that the staff was keeping everything clean. Wall panels were scuffed from abuse and once beautiful tapestries and draperies were heavy with dirt or removed entirely from the vaulted windows. There were no homey touches anywhere leaving a barren, sterile environment. She imagined that the Magician didn't waste too much money on palace maintenance. It fueled her anger against the man who had destroyed her happy life.

Their goal was the third floor toward the back of the palace that overlooked the gardens. With each step, they expected to come upon someone- a guard or soldier. The neglect continued and the air hung with the heavy smell of dust and mildew. They reached the floor they wanted without encountering anyone and paused to get their bearings.

"Which way do we go now?" Angeline asked.

The two guards were scanning the hall in both directions and listening for any sound that would indicate someone approaching. One of them cautioned them to stay where they were until he could check out the room where Prince Alair might be. The other guard stayed with them and pulled a wicked-looking knife out from under his tunic. He pressed them close to the wall and kept his eyes on the hallway. The first guard wasn't gone long.

"The first room is empty but I can hear a sound in the other room. The door is locked but, when we get you in there, we can open that, by force if necessary. Follow closely."

They made their way quickly and quietly to the room, carefully opened the door, and entered. They were in a room furnished as a sitting room with a cluster of seating around the cheery fire. This room showed more life and care. Across the room, a carved wooden door led to another room. Rose knew that this suite was normally reserved for visiting dignitaries. It was well away from the family suite, a set of rooms she imagined had been commandeered for the Magician's personal use. They were beautiful rooms and much too grand for such a swine. Rose realized that she needed to get herself under control. She would do Alair no good if she didn't remain calm.

Angeline strode to the locked door and placed her ear on the wood panel. She listened but couldn't distinguish the origin of the sound that she could hear. The Magician had placed a ward on the door so that no but he could enter. She let her hand hover over the door handle and lock. She focused her mind on the elements involved. She encountered a powerful seal and stepped back so as not to alert the Magician to his ward being explored.

"We need to shield what we do so that the Magician doesn't become aware of our presence. He has a powerful ward on this door. The three of us have to work together. Rose, I will have you move the mechanism in the door when I call on you. Amey, I want you to find the path that your mother will follow while I cloak what we are doing. Do not hurry. We cannot risk him becoming suspicious"

Amey moved to her grandmother's side. Rose moved and knelt quietly in front of the door and was poised waiting for the signal. Angeline described what they would be doing and how she wanted Amey to proceed. Amey grasped her amulet and felt the powerful pull of the stones. She let herself sink into the power and waited for her grandmother's signal. She felt the shield go up around them. Rose concentrated on keeping the elements of the lock stable while Amey sent her mind forward into the lock mechanism. It was like walking down steel corridors, turning this way and that and leaving a glowing trail behind. When she passed through the lock tumblers, she summoned her mother.

Rose slowly and carefully followed Amey's path. When she reached her daughter, she moved aside the pieces and was startled by the deafening 'click' they made. She knew no one could hear but it still made her nervous. At last, the pieces were manipulated to their open position and Rose and Amey eased back. The lock was in the open position but the ward needed to be taken down before they could open the door. Mother and daughter viewed the ward and saw that it was a simple 'hold' spell and proceeded carefully to remove it. When they were sure that they hadn't left anything for the Magician to sense, they backed out and Angeline released her shield.

When she reached for the handle to open the door, the guard stopped her saying,

"Let me do that, milady. We don't know what is on the other side."

Knife in hand, he turned the knob and pushed the door open so he could look inside. He tilled his head from side to side to search for any danger. The room was dim and he saw nothing to alarm him. He pushed it open farther and they all entered. This was the bedchamber and was occupied by a massive four-poster bed that was screened by heavy curtains. The sounds that they heard were coming from there. They walked around the foot of the bed and pulled aside the hangings. Lying there on top of the covers, propped on pillows, was a pale man with long, black hair and vacant dark blue eyes mumbling a phrase that they couldn't make out. He was dressed in a simple shirt and casual pants but his feet were bare. He hadn't aged much in the last seventeen years except that he was thinner but not gaunt. It was as if he hadn't had much exercise to keep him fit but he didn't appear to be ill. A sob broke from Rose's throat and her mother hugged her close. Amey pressed forward to get her first view of her father.

"Oh, Alair, what has he done to you? "

Angeline moved her daughter aside and reached out a hand to touch his forehead. She leaned closer and tried to understand what he was murmuring but could understand. She closed her eyes and reached into his mind. What she found was locked away behind a dark barricade. She'd felt the same blockage in the young boy, Perrin but nowhere near as strong. It would have to be stronger for a grown man. She tried to find out the extent but couldn't go past. She didn't find any noticeable damage but couldn't be sure.

'Amey, see if you can find out what is holding him?"

Amey was hesitant about approaching the man who was her father. She looked at his face and could see herself written there. He looked too young to be her father though but she never doubted it because of her mother's reaction. She looked over at her grandmother and received a nod of encouragement. Her mother still stared at the man on the bed.

Amey moved forward to her father's side. She lifted her left hand to his forehead, grasped her pendant with the other, and closed her eyes. She sought the power and the light and reached into it to let it engulf her. She extended its reach out to her father and explored the barricade. It was a strong barrier, stronger than the one she encountered with Perrin. She felt sadness and desolation. Searching carefully, Amey pried at the edges of the wall and found it held tight but she was able to decipher the nature of the block. She could see some of the images that ran through his mind in an endless loop and hear what he was continually saying. As she listened, bitter hatred filled her and she had to gain control over her emotions. She backed out carefully and surfaced to find both her grandmother and mother watching her closely. She knew they saw the anger on her face and couldn't do anything to hide it. She felt deeply saddened.

"What is it, Amey? What did you see? Were you able to get in?" her mother said.

Rose grabbed hold of her hands, clasping them tightly. Amey needed time to get her emotions in check. She looked from one to the other and chose her words carefully.

"He has used a similar approached with my father as he did with Perrin. Perhaps that's why he used it on the little boy because it is so effective. The block is stronger. He has planted images in his mind and they play continuously and have taken his will to live. They relate to what he is saying also."

Her Mother held on to her hands with renewed vigor.

"What images, Amey. What could he possible show to make Alair not want to live?"

Amey looked into her mother's eyes. She knew she had to tell her but it pained her to add to her mother's distress. She looked to her grandmother and saw her eyes narrow as she moved to hold her daughter closer to ease the blow that was to come. She nodded to Amey.

"I saw what the Magician placed in his mind. He plays an image across his brain like a movie showing his parents death. Part of the image shows who had arranged for it to happen while the rest indicates that same person betraying him. It shows him being laughed at and being called a fool behind his back. On top of his parent's death, this betrayal broke his spirit."

Rose turned in her mother's arms and cried,

"Oh, Mother, what a horrible thing to do to someone. We have to stop this."

Angeline looked into her granddaughter's eyes and read there the extent of the horror.

"Rose, I think there's more Amey needs to tell you. Go ahead, Amey."

Amey breathed in deeply and let it out slowly. She hated what she had to say next.

"You are the person showed betraying my father, laughing at him and calling him a fool for thinking you were in love with him. He cries and mourns at the same time and cannot imagine why he should continue living. He keeps saying in his mind "She never loved me. She never loved me."

Amey fell silent and watched the horror fully dawn on her mother.

"No. No! How could he think that? How could he believe that? Mother, how could he think that?"

"Oh Rose, Alair was in shock from his parent's deaths and the Magician took advantage of it. He worked with that grief and used his mind control power to plant the image. Alair was susceptible. Amey, can you get through the barricade as you did with Perrin?"

"It is a very strong one, Grandmother. I will try but I can't be sure. I could barely pry an edge up to see what I did."

"You can only try. Gentlemen, can you please pull back the bed curtains and lower the prince flat on his back? Rose, pull yourself together. We need to work as quickly as possible. We need your powers as well as ours. You and I will hold a barrier against the Magician sensing what we are doing.

The prince was laid flat on the bed. Amey pulled the small pack from under her cloak. She opened it on the bedside table and separated the stones into groups. She turned to the bed and positioned her father's head so that it was even. She turned his palms upward and had to close her mind to the fact that this was her father so that she could concentrate on the ritual. She grasped her amulet and sought a meditative state. With the help of the selection of stones she had fashioned together, she reached down into the center of her being and prayed fervently for the power to help her father. A strong light began to form and quickly engulfed her. She reveled in it and let it fill her.

Amey placed the crystals on his chest with the largest that Bear Claw Mt. had given her closest to his heart. She arranged the supporting gemstones on his palms and then lifted the banded amethyst. It glowed and sparkled in the light from the windows and she placed it in the center of his forehead. She held it there with her left hand and lifted her right hand to her amulet and crystal pendant gripping them together against her chest. The room was quiet except for their breath and the murmur from her father. Amey reached down into the glowing pool of light and felt it pulse. It grew brighter and brighter. It shone like a hundred white suns. When Amey thought she couldn't stand the brightness any longer, she pushed the energy through her arm to the gemstone on her father's brow. She reached into his mind and tried to coax the barrier aside. It wouldn't move. She called out to him. "Alair. Alair" and received no answer. Amey called on her powers and grasped the barrier trying to rend it from its place. Nothing worked.

She had to regroup but she couldn't think what she could do next. How could she reach him? A thought came to her. It seemed simple enough but she knew it would be harder than it seemed. She reached into her power and began to create images. She expanded the images and stretched them into a story. She strengthened the images with sounds and created her own movie. When it was almost complete, Amey added in something at the last minute. She fed it into the crack in the barrier. It pushed aside the Magician's images and played over Alair's mind. After viewing it a few times, Amey felt a change in her father's consciousness. It was as if he were sitting up and taking an interest in the new display. She reached out again and gripped the barrier. This time she held on and recalled the ritual prayer.

Through your healing Stones of Power
By my willing hand,

Open up the shuttered mind
Remove constraining bands.
Let your healing Light
Free the shackled mind,
Free the fettered spirit,
Leaving bonds behind.

A burst of awesome power surged through her and she felt the barrier weaken. She repeated the prayer and again felt the power race through her and crash against the wall. Amey felt it weaken further. Drawing on every ounce of power she possessed, she recited the prayer a third time.

Through your healing Stones of Power
By my willing hand,
Open up the shuttered mind
Remove constraining bands.
Let your healing Light
Free the shackled mind,
Free the fettered spirit,
Leaving bonds behind.

Blazing power battered the wall of the barricade and crumbled it. Amey reached through calling,

"Alair. Alair! Father! Reach out to me. Let me help you. I am your daughter, Amey."

Alair seemed to be coming out of a dream. He reached out to the image of Amey in his mind and held on. He was in awe.

"My daughter? I have a daughter? My lovely daughter?"

Alair smiled and lapsed into peaceful rest. Amey gradually eased back, letting the light spread in her body. She stood quietly awhile and finally opened her eyes. She felt her face break into a smile.

"I just met my father," she said and hugged her mother.

Angeline wiped tears from her eyes and broke into the happy moment. As much as she cherished this moment, there wasn't any time to waste. She spoke the word 'release' and Rose followed suit.

"Rose, we should attempt to heal Alair. He needs to recover so that we can leave here quickly."

They went about the planned ritual and used their combined force to work off the remaining effects of the Magician's evil. They worked quickly and were rewarded when they saw colour return to Alair's skin. Within moments, he opened his eyes and looked from one person to the next. His gaze lingered on Rose and his eyes filled with tears. She went and held his hand to her breast and smiled through her tears. He reached up his other hand and caressed her cheek.

"Rose, my Rose. I had the most horrible nightmare."

"Yes, I know, my darling, I know."

Alair turned his head and looked at Amey. He was somewhat confused.

"I know you. You're Amey. You're my daughter! We have a daughter, Rose?"

"Oh yes, Alair, we have a daughter. A beautiful, clever daughter."

Angeline leaned forward and took Alair's hand urging him to sit. The guards brought a pair of shoes they'd found and bent to place them at his feet.

"Here are your shoes, sire," they both said and bowed.

"Come, Alair. We need to get away from here. We are not safe. Are you well enough?"

Alair stood up carefully. He seemed to be checking himself out in his mind.

"I think so. Why do we need to go away?"

"We can't explain to you now. Come with us and we will tell you all you want to know."

Rose knelt and took the shoes and helped Alair put them on.

"Thank you.

"Wait a minute"

Amey reached into her bag and pulled out another amulet she'd made at the last minute before they left the Lodge.

"Will you wear this father? I made it to protect you."

"I will be proud to wear what you've made me."

He put the amulet around his neck and carefully stood. He didn't feel too bad. A little weak, perhaps, but still able to function well enough. He must've been sick. The guards stepped toward the door and out into the next room. The rest followed close behind. When they were all assembled, the guard opened the door to the hall.

"Where are we going?" Alair asked.

"We are going down to the kitchens, sire. We need to be careful so as not to be seen. We will leave the palace from there."

Alair looked around to see where they were. He got his bearings and made a suggestion.

"There's another way down to the kitchens. Let me show you. It isn't a way that is used because it is very narrow and not convenient. It also isn't widely known to exist. We will not be observed this way," he said with a twinkle in his eye.

The group exchanged looks and decided in an instant.

"Show us the way, Alair. We will follow you."

Angeline spoke with confidence and Alair nodded his head. He'd grown up in this palace and knew every nook and cranny. This was the way he chose to sneak down to raid the pantry when he was a small boy. He moved over to a large floor to ceiling painting of some long past battle and released the catch on the frame. The picture swung out revealing a narrow stairway. It was dark in the passageway. Angeline pulled her crystal from her garment and told Rose and Amey to do likewise. Their power caused their crystals to glow with a soft light that lit their way. They wound down the stairs. You could tell by the dust that they hadn't been used in years. Slowly and quietly, they made their way. At each floor, you could see the back of another painting. Finally, they reached the bottom. Alair released the hidden catch and stepped back to let a guard ease the door open a crack to see if anyone was around. When he was satisfied that no one was near, he let Alair out to lead the way. As a group, they headed for the kitchen which was a short distance around a corner. Just as the last guard had closed the door and turned to follow the rest of the group, a small patrol of the Magician's men came into the hall. They yelled and started running down the hall toward them.

"Stop! You there, stop"

Angeline ran towards the safety of the kitchen with the others close behind. She could see the cook had come to the doorway and was urging them to hurry. The rest of the kitchen staff were ranged behind him holding various kitchen utensils and pots as weapons. As they came through the doorway they were moved aside and the cook stood to the side of the doorway with a heavy skillet opposite his helper who wielded a massive rolling pin.

The two guards who hung back to protect the group came backing down the stairs to the kitchen. When they reached the last step, the kitchen staff pushed them after the escaping family. The cook held up his cast iron frying pan while the others gripped whatever weapon they had. A beefy woman wielded a second polished wooden rolling pin, another a meat mallet, still another held a thick ironstone jug.

"Go on. Catch up to our prince and the queen and get them away safely. We'll take care of them."

When the patrol burst into the kitchen, they were met with a barrage of blows and fell before they could defend themselves. The kitchen staff trussed them up and put them in the storage room with gags in their mouths, leaving someone there to keep an eye on them. The rest of the staff brushed off their hands and grinned at each other. The cook reached into the cupboard and brought out a jug of cider.

'I think this calls for a drink. Grab a mug everyone," and he poured each of them a hearty round.

"To the Prince," he said and raised his mug high and everyone followed.

"To the prince and down with the Magician!"

Chapter Fourteen –Reunited

The fighting in the city wound down. The citizens captured and caged as many as two hundred and fifty of the enemy. They were being held out of the city in secure buildings warded against discovery and guarded by elders with considerable powers but who were getting too old to fight. Everyone was doing their part. The Magician was marshalling his remaining men to stage an attack in force against the loyalists and was drawing his scattered forces back from the search of the countryside. Everyone was preparing as best they could for the assault that was sure to come in the next few hours at the earliest but surely by the next morning.

Jasper and Lirin met up somewhere along the line. They stayed behind in the city to wait and offer any assistance they could to Angeline, Rose and Amey. Should they be able to release the prince, they would be there to help them escape. In a vacant livery stable, they had a speedy carriage and horses waiting. They anxiously watched the palace.

They heard an alarm ring out at the same time as the kitchen entrance burst open and the three women and the guards ran out. With them was a very thin but obviously alive and aware Prince Alair. They reached Jasper and Lirin who hurried them away to the stable. The guards mounted the horses while everyone else piled into the carriage. Lirin took the driver's bench and urged the carriage horses into action. As they pulled away, they could hear the sounds of pursuit. They were purposely heading in the wrong direction. They did not want to lead the Magician's forces to their doorstep. They were heading into the border country and would cross over it to throw off the pursuit. There would be fresh horses waiting for them. Once changed, they would continue in a circuitous route back to the Lodge. They had lots of work to do to deploy their own people for the fight to come.

Inside the carriage, everyone sat back in relief to catch their breath. They looked around at each other and started to speak at the same time. After the initial surprise this caused, they collapsed in laughter. They wiped the happy tears from their eyes and Jasper took hold of the situation and said,

"Welcome, my prince. I'm so pleased to see you safe, milord. I see your rescue was a success. What happened?" He asked questions about the rescue to the group but the prince replied,

"Jasper! It is good to see you also but I'm afraid that I am at a loss how to answer your question. Perhaps Queen Angeline would be the best one to give you the answer."

Angeline sat up and composed herself. She still had a smile on her face.

"You will be pleased to know, Alair, that your palace staff have remained loyal to you all these years."

"All these years? You need to explain what has been happening. I have vague memories that don't make any sense and, add to that, now I have a grown daughter I knew nothing about."

Rose put her arm through her husband's arm. There was so much to tell him but where to begin?

"Alair, do you remember when we were married?"

"Of course! It was the happiest day of my life. We went on a wonderful honeymoon but it was interrupted by the death of my parents and we had to return."

A frown creased his forehead as if he were trying to remember. Fragments of images came into his mind and he looked to his wife in surprise and uncertainty.

"Before you say anything, let me tell you what I remember. I remember how happy we were and how it shook you when the message came that your parents were dead. We arrived home to find your cousin Balik waiting and he said, being older, he should take you under his wing. He occupied your time, took over the funeral arrangements, and pushed me aside. Soon, he had you looking at me strangely and I found out he had plans that I couldn't tolerate. I tried to warn you but he had some sort of control over you. So, I ran to my mother and found that there had been an attempt on her life at the same time as your parents were killed. We found out your cousin had arranged for the murder attempt and we believe he did the same to your parents. We received a warning that he would try again and escaped just before men came to kill both of us."

"Amey told us what she saw in your mind when she broke his hold on you. Your cousin is a powerful, evil magician and he put you in a trance or held your mind in some way. He put horrible thoughts and images in your mind until Amey replaced them with the truth."

She reached up and placed her palm against his cheek. She looked deeply, searchingly into his eyes. She spoke softly with great emotion.

"My love, I couldn't betray you any more than I could stop breathing. When we realized Balik controlled you, we didn't know what we could do to save you. I found out after we escaped that I was carrying your baby and keeping it safe was the most important priority. We knew when Amey was born that she had amazing powers. We started planning to rescue you then but your cousin had taken control and had a vicious group of men in his employ. Many people were watching over you for us. Now we have you here."

Rose continued to watch his face to see how he reacted to what she'd told him. He looked torn and uncertain. He turned his head and looked at Amey. He couldn't deny that she was his daughter as it was like looking in the mirror to see her. She took his hand in both of hers and hugged them to her.

"I just found out about you, Father, but I know what Mother says about your cousin is true. He is cruel and evil. I had to save a young boy from the images he'd placed in his mind- images that terrified a ten-year-old boy so much that he hid inside himself away from his family. He did that simply because the boy had tried to keep him from taking his father and because he could."

She reached up and placed her hand over the protection amulet she'd made. She had included a piece of fluorite because it could lessen any psychic control that the Magician had over her father.

"Here, put your hand over mine while I hold this amulet. Let me help you see clearly."

Slowly, Alair placed his hand over Amey's and clasped it firmly. Amey closed her eyes and willed herself to summon the Light. It came quickly and filled her with its singing brightness. She opened her mind and reached for her father. She bathed him in its healing power and soothed his doubt and uncertainty. She played for him scenes from her childhood and she felt him relax. She saw the beginning of peace and happiness enfold him. When she opened her eyes, Amey saw the wonder in his. He smiled at her lovingly and turned to his wife with the smile still in place.

"I see clearly now. I'm so sorry for what has happened and all the time together we've lost."

"We'll make up for it now. That is, as soon as we can remove your cousin from power. He won't go without a fight but we are as ready as we can be."

Angeline watched the transformation with satisfaction. Jasper was pleased also, but still wanted to know what had happened in the palace. Angeline took up the story again.

"The kitchen staff were wonderful. They got us into the palace and hid us until we could hear fighting in the city. Your diversion worked well and our guards led us through the palace to the room where they believed we'd find Alair. Once there, Amey reached into Alair's mind to determine how strongly he was being controlled. She returned and told us just what the Magician had placed there. We were horrified! Amey then set up the ritual and, as we watched, she sought to reach through the barricade to her father. We saw the same light move through her as we saw with Perrin but this time it filled her body, not just her arm and flowed into Alair. The crystal she brought from the mountain also glowed brightly. We could see the struggle she waged against the control. Finally, whatever she was doing appeared to work and we could see Alair coming back to us."

"The Magician had planted cruel images of betrayal and deceit. He made it look like Mother was behind his parent's deaths and didn't love him. I replaced the images that the Magician had created with the true story. As a final step, I introduced myself."

Amey blushed a little. Jasper laughed in amazement and Angeline smiled fondly at her granddaughter. Rose reached over with her free hand and held Amey's.

Angeline continued,

"Very inventive! Anyway, once Rose and I were able to help Alair recover so that we could get away, we followed a secret route back to the kitchen that he showed us. Our luck had held until then but we were seen by a patrol just as we were about to escape through the kitchen. The guards hung back to allow us time but the kitchen staff pushed them after us saying they would take care of the rest. I looked back in time to see the cook, Oscar, bring this massive cast iron frying pan down on the heads of a couple of the men as they came into the kitchen. What a sight! We'll have to reward him in some way. The rest of the staff had rolling pins and other implements and bashed heads as they rushed into the kitchen. From there, we ran out of the palace into your arms and here we are. What happened in the city?"

"Our plan worked out well also. We have as many as two hundred and fifty of the Magician's men caged and being held by the elders. We sustained some serious injuries but no deaths. We took them completely by surprise and were able to bring them down quickly. The carts hauled them away and they shouldn't give us any more trouble. We need to get back, though, because the Magician isn't going to wait to try to overpower the loyalists."

"May I join you?"

Alair's question turned every eye toward him. Jasper considered the request and said,

"Are you sure you are well enough? Do you really want to fight against a member of your family?"

Alair didn't hesitate. The colour had come back into his face and he appeared stronger. His expression turned hard,

"Did it concern Balik that it was family when he killed my parents? I loved my parents dearly and I couldn't live with myself if I didn't avenge their deaths. I cannot forgive him for the years he has robbed from me and our family or the tyranny over my people"

"Alright, when we get back, we will fill you in on all our plans. You know this country better than any of us. The people who were hesitant to join us against the Magician will rethink their position when they see you. They will rally around you as the true head of government. We need all the support we can get."

They arrived at the appointed exchange and the horses were switched. Jasper gave the two guards instructions concerning the coming battle and sent them off to various posts. After a break where everyone got out of the carriage and stretched their legs, they climbed back in ready for the last stage of the journey. They proceeded with extreme care as they were going into more settled territory. The Magician had spies everywhere. Angeline and Jasper set wards around their carriage so that they wouldn't be discovered easily but still they proceeded quickly but cautiously.

It took them more than three hours to get back. They wanted to stop in the town to ensure their plans were being carried out but parked the carriage first in a secluded spot. Lirin said,

"I will go on ahead to see if it is safe for you."

They again climbed down to stretch and waited until Lirin returned with news. After a half hour when he didn't return, Jasper decided it would be best to carry on to the Lodge by foot through the forest. He was worried about Alair but didn't want to embarrass him by suggesting he wasn't up to the walk. He looked to Angeline who appeared to be thinking along the same lines. The weather had cleared but there was still a damp chill in the air and Alair had been confined for a long time.

"Alair, do you think you can walk the two miles or so it will take to make it to the Lodge?"

Alair wasn't insulted but more introspective. He seemed to be checking out his body with his mind to see if he could make the trip.

"I feel good. I don't think I'm weak or sickly. Yes, I think I can make it. If I find it too arduous, I can always sit down and rest. Let's get on our way."

Angeline was convinced by the prince's positive attitude. They unhitched the team of horses and picketed them out. They would send someone back to collect them later. They gathered their belongings and started to walk in a wide circle around the town. The forest was lovely with spring growth. The rain had freshened the air and the tang of the evergreens flowed softly over their faces. Under any other circumstances, they would've enjoyed the walk, but they were worried about Lirin. As soon as they were well past the town, Jasper spoke to Angeline and left them to head back to the town.

"Jasper is going to see about Lirin. He told us to go on without him."

Amey had worried also on the walk. Lirin had been a vital support in her first days and had built her confidence by his humour and confidence in her abilities. He was someone she could relate to and in whom she could confide her fears. He had quickly become her friend.

"Jasper, wait." Amey spoke quickly to her grandmother and parents. "I want to go with him. Maybe I can help."

Her Mother immediately said "No" but her grandmother was instead considering her wish. She looked at Rose and cautioned her,

"Rose, we knew when Amey was born that she would do great things. Already her power has released Alair. This is something she needs to do and I think we need to let her go. Jasper will protect her and she can also protect herself."

Rose was torn. She looked to Alair and he nodded his head. Rose gave in and gave Amey a fierce hug.

"You take care! Follow Jasper's lead. I know you won't do anything foolish, but just remember how worried we will be and hurry back."

"I will. Thank you."

Amey ran after Jasper who was waiting for her. She turned and gave a jaunty wave and followed him deeper into the woods.

On their walk back to the lodge, Angeline and Rose surreptitiously kept an eye on Alair to gauge his fitness. He seems to strengthen with each step and they arrived at the lodge in a short time. Lookouts had announced their approach. Nanny Pearl was waiting in the doorway on the porch with the other lodge residents standing on and around the porch in anticipation of the rescue having worked. When they saw the prince with Angeline and Rose, they shouted their joy.

"Hooray! Welcome back, milord! Your majesty, welcome home!"

Nanny Pearl bowed to the prince and then ushered them in. In typical Nanny Pearl fashion, she took charge.

"Now you let Nanny Pearl take care of you. Can I make you something to eat, your majesty. Would you like a tea, sir, or should I bring out something a little stronger?" she said. "Oh dear, whatever am I thinking! Get yourself into the parlour and get comfortable. You look like you need some fattening up, sir, and I will make something good and hearty to start. Rose, see to your husband!"

She whirled away. As they left the kitchen, Alair stopped to watch Nanny Pearl bustling around the kitchen pulling open cupboards and taking out pots and pans.

"She hasn't changed a bit although she used to call me a scallywag or sometimes an imp or rascal then feed me all sorts of goodies. I hope she loses the 'sir' because it just doesn't sound right. Something to work on."

Jasper and Amey walked quickly and carefully, keeping their eyes trained for anything out of place. As they neared the town, they couldn't hear any sound. The woods ended on the edge of the people's gardens. Jasper and Amey stopped to listen for sounds of danger and moved ahead carefully to the back of a house that bordered the town square. They edged their way along the wall to a large bush on the corner of the building. Its new spring growth offered them shelter without blocking their view. What they saw surprised them.

The street was empty but, at the far end, there was a crowd that was utterly silent. Seeing no one else around, Jasper and Amey hurried forward to see what was wrong. Jasper pushed his way through the crowd and Amey followed in his wake. There, on the ground, with blood flowing from a head wound and a knife wound in his shoulder lay Lirin. He had been hastily covered with someone's cloak and another was rolled up under his head. Jasper knelt quickly and checked his pulse. Amey knelt on the other side and took his free hand. The door of the house behind them burst open and a woman named Abigail rushed down the stairs with an armload of cloths. Following behind came a young girl carrying a bucket of hot water. They rushed to where Lirin was lying.

Jasper looked up and demanded,

"What happened here?"

"Oh Jasper, the Magician's men were here a while ago and they were harassing everyone. My daughter here was out to hang the clothes on the line for me. The men surrounded her and started to push her back and forth between them. They were getting rougher and rougher all the time and my daughter was crying. Just then, Lirin walked into town and saw what was happening. He hurried over and pulled away one of the men telling them to leave her alone. As a group they turned on him. One man held him while the others took turns punching him."

Jasper pulled aside the cloak covering him and lifted Lirin's tunic. His body was covered with red patches that were rapidly turning to bruises. He ran his hands carefully over his torso to see if anything was broken. He couldn't find anything obvious but didn't doubt that there might be more serious injuries found on closer inspection. Lirin stirred.

"Lie still, boy," said Jasper.

Jasper looked over to Amey silently asking her to keep Lirin calm and still. Amey reached under her cloak and clutched her crystal. She willed peace and calm to fill her shaken body. She let that peace and calm flow into Lirin and saw him relax.

Jasper moved aside to make room for Abigail to tend Lirin. He took out his knife and cut away the shirt from the wounded shoulder. Abigail dipped the cloth in the hot water and washed away the blood. Jasper was happy to see that the wound wasn't as serious as he thought it might be- more a deep scratch than a penetrating wound. She made a pad of another clean cloth and pressed it onto the seeping gash.

"Can you hold this in place, please?"

Rinsing her cloth, she wiped the blood off Lirin's face and forehead. The cut here would require stitches. Reaching into her apron, Abigail threaded clean cotton through a curved needle and pulled the ragged edges of the wound together. She looked up at Jasper and asked,

"Can you keep his head steady, Jasper? He cannot move while I stitch the wound."

Jasper leaned over and placed his hands on either side of Lirin's head. He again looked at Amey and she sought to keep Lirin calm. She focused her power and fed it to Lirin. He remained relaxed and peaceful while Abigail closed the gash.

"Why were the Magician's men here?"

Abigail continued to work but answered,

"I don't think they had any reason. They've been coming around more often lately. Our men are staying closer to town so they can protect us better."

"That's likely what they want. Where did his attackers go?"

"I heard my daughter crying and came out yelling at them to leave her alone. When our men saw what was happening, several of them came to Lirin's rescue. They chased them away and some followed to make sure that they kept going. They aren't back yet."

Abigail ripped a long strip off one of the cloths. She wrapped it around Lirin's head over another cloth pad. The shoulder wound had stopped bleeding but the pad was left in place anyway. Jasper helped get the cloth strip under the shirt so it could be tied to keep it secure. He looked around the crowd.

"John, we left a carriage and horses in the poplar clearing outside of town. Could you please go and hitch up the team and bring it here so we can get Lirin home?"

"Sure, Jasper. I won't be long."

While he hurried away, Jasper and a few of the men went to put together a stretcher of some sort. Amey followed for a short distance to ask Jasper,

"Do you think it would help if I tried to see if there were any serious injuries?"

Jasper was distracted and angry. He turned to Amey and fought to control himself.

"I think that's a good idea. Thank you. I'm not thinking clearly. Perhaps there might even be something you can do to hasten his healing."

He stopped talking and just stared into space. When he spoke again, Amey had to listen closely as he spoke quietly.

"I thought he was dead! I thought I'd lost him too." He turned a ravaged face to Amey. "He's all that I have left."

He turned and hurried away and Amey knew his pain. She'd also thought him dead. She felt so relieved when she'd felt his pulse. She thought she'd lost him too. She went back to Lirin. Most of the crowd had dispersed but Abigail and her daughter were still there.

"Hi, I'm Abigail and this is my daughter Sarah. You're Queen Angeline's granddaughter, aren't you?"

It was still a shock to hear her grandmother called 'queen' but Amey offered her hand in greeting.

"Yes, I am. My name is Amey. Nice to meet you too, Sarah."

Amey knelt down beside Lirin.

"If you don't mind, I'd like to just sit here a short while with Lirin. I don't want to chase you away. I am going to offer up a prayer for him"

She took his hand and closed her eyes. Her hand reached under her cloak and grasped her amulet. She breathed in and out, following her breath and called for the Light. She felt its brilliance and reached out with it to Lirin. She tracked the call of his pain, visiting each site and determining its severity. While there, she sought to lessen that pain. Once she'd satisfied herself that there were no major injuries, Amey concentrated on healing the ones that were there. The shoulder wound didn't require much effort but the gash on his head was more involved. She focused the healing light on the task and bathed the wound much as Abigail did with water. Having done all she could, Amey withdrew and sat quietly at his side.

Lirin's eyelids fluttered and gradually opened. Amey smiled at him and received one in return. He went to sit up and Amey pressed a hand to his chest to stop him.

"Lie still. You've been injured and the carriage will be here soon to take us home."

Lirin lay back. He winced at the pain the movement caused.

"I was really stupid," he said, disgusted with himself. He continued, "Who in their right mind tries to take on armed men single-handed?"

Amey agreed but offered instead soothing sounds. She turned to watch Jasper come up. He knelt down quickly when he saw Lirin awake.

"How are you feeling? Haven't I taught you anything, boy? What got into you, taking on armed men when you were outnumbered?"

Amey reached across and touched Jasper's arm.

"He was just saying what a stupid thing it was to do. I'm just happy he's alive."

Jasper blew out his breath and relaxed. He looked at Lirin.

"Yes, so am I. So am I."

"I found no serious injuries, Jasper. He has lots of aching spots and the cut on his head will turn into a magnificent headache in a while. I think it will be safe to move him."

"Well then, let's see if we can sit you up safely."

He put his arm behind his shoulders and eased him into a sitting position. You could see the effort flit across Lirin's face but he didn't make a sound. When in an upright position, he took deep, steadying breaths until he felt comfortable.

John drove up with the carriage and jumped down to help Jasper steady Lirin on his feet. The men who came up with Jasper set aside the makeshift litter and held open the door while one stepped in the carriage to help lift Lirin from the inside. Abigail brought a blanket and wrapped it around him and said quietly,

"Thank you for helping my daughter, Lirin. I'm sorry you had to get hurt in the process."

Jasper helped her from the carriage.

"I want to thank you, Abigail, for the care you've given my nephew. He's important to me."

"As is my daughter to me. You are welcome, Jasper."

Amey climbed in beside Lirin while Jasper mounted to the driver's seat.

"After I get these two home, I'll be back to talk to the men when they return.

He flicked the reins and headed the horses to the Lodge. In the carriage, Amey and Lirin rode in companionable silence.

"Amey, what did you do back there?"

She looked over at Lirin.

"How did you know I did anything?"

"I remember being in the dark, in pain and feeling adrift. Then there was a brilliant light and I didn't feel lost anymore. The pain was still there but, every time I felt it, the light would wash over it and it would ease. I can tell you I still ache but it would've been worse if you hadn't done something. I don't think I could've stood up as I did."

"I merely used the light to find out if you had any major internal injuries. While I was there, I eased any pains that I found."

"Well, thank you for whatever you did. I definitely worked."

They sat quietly, rocking gently in the swaying carriage. The more Amey learned; the more questions were raised in her mind.

"Lirin, what can you do with your power?"

"What do you mean?"

Amey half-turned in the seat to face him.

"I know so little about the power even after all the lessons. Every time I do something with it, I wonder what else I can do. I haven't learned most of the actions I've been able to do. Like with you just now. I didn't know what I was going to do. When I called on the light, I just did what seemed logical and searched out your injuries and eased your pain. Have you done that before? Can you heal?"

Lirin was looking tired but he answered as well as he could.

"I know that there are different degrees of power. I also know that extreme situations enable people to do amazing things. I can heal injuries but I haven't been called on to do anything more. I don't know what is possible to do with the power. I'll just keep watching you and learn as you keep exploring the possibilities."

Amey saw how hard it was for Lirin to concentrate. She sat back and rested his head on her shoulder.

"Have a nap and when we are almost there, I will wake you up. No one will need to know."

She pulled the blanket up around him and tucked it in securely. He nestled his head on her shoulder and was soon asleep. Amey spent the remaining time thinking about the possibilities and what was to come next.

Chapter Fifteen – Rally

Nanny Pearl took over as soon as they arrived at the Lodge. She bowed to the prince respectfully and then waved them away brusquely turning to the injured young man. Lirin was whisked away with Nanny Pearl scolding, soothing, and questioning all at the same time. Jasper wanted to go with them but lagged behind to escape the brunt of the tirade. He cast them a last pained look before they disappeared around the corner to Lirin's quarters.

"What happened," asked Angeline?

"Lirin walked into the town just as the Magician's men were harassing a young girl named Sarah. He stepped in to stop them and they turned on him."

Amey told her grandmother about them finding Lirin on the ground covered in blood.

"We thought he was dead!"

She told how shaken Jasper was.

"He said, 'I thought I lost him too.' Lirin's pretty badly beaten. He also has a small knife wound in his shoulder. Sarah's mother, Abigail, bathed and stitched his wounds while Jasper held him steady. He wanted me to keep him calm so I used the crystal. I wanted to help so I tried to see how injured he was. I followed his pain and found he didn't have anything broken. I eased his aches as much as I could. I guess it helped because Lirin woke up and was able to get to his feet with help. Jasper sent someone for the carriage and we brought him home."

"Did you find out what the Magician's men were doing there?"

'Abigail said that they had been coming around more often lately and the men were staying close to home to keep watch. Jasper thought that might be why they were doing it- to keep the men close to home and away from any fighting."

Angeline nodded her head in agreement.

"I think he's right. Come on now. Let's go find your mother and father. They are in the livingroom, I think."

Angeline led Amey to the comfortable room where Rose and Alair were seated side by side on the sofa by the fire. Rose silently held out her hand to Amey and she went over and sat on the floor at their feet. They were looking at an old photo album that showed Amey as a child. Alair would pause from time to time and run a slender fingertip over the face of the picture. He looked overwhelmed. Amey had never seen the album before.

"Where did that come from?" she asked.

Rose smiled and said,

"Your grandmother brought it here years ago so she could look at you when she was away from the farm."

Amey looked over at her grandmother who was reading from a stack of papers and smiled at the thought of her grandmother sitting, just as she was now and looking at the photo album. It dawned on Amey that her father's reaction might have as much to do with the fact that he had never seen a photograph before as it had to do with the pictures themselves. He was totally engrossed in the images.

"I've been telling your father all about our earlier life; about the farm and the fact that Bear Claw Mt. is there too."

Alair looked up from the album. He had obviously been listening to their conversation.

"Here it is called Cléa. I believe, in the old language, it means 'claw.' You chose your name for it well."

He looked down at the album. He spoke with so much sadness and bitterness.

"I've missed all this. You carrying my child, Amey's birth, her growing up. I've missed it all. No, I won't have any trouble fighting against Balik. None at all!"

Amey reached out and placed her hand over her father's.

"You won't have to miss anything anymore."

Jasper entered the room and all eyes turned to him.

"He's going to be alright. Nanny told him he's lucky to have such a hard head. I didn't have to tell him anything. He's too busy blaming himself for being so stupid. Nanny Pearl won't let him out of bed, though. He has orders to stay there and not get up before tomorrow morning. With all his bruises, he's not going to be moving too quickly even then. He can probably ease most of the effects himself when he thinks about it but I'll probably take pity on him later and add to the treatment."

Jasper went over to a big, overstuffed chair on the other side of the fire and sank into it gratefully, putting his head back and closing his eyes. Angeline poured a small glass of brandy from the decanter on the table and brought it over to him.

"Take this. You look like you could use it."

Jasper lifted his head and opened his eyes. He accepted the glass and took a sip. The warmth spread through him to all the cold spots left by the fear of losing Lirin.

"Thank you. I needed that. This incident scared me. Lirin means everything to me. I thought I'd lost him. I panicked."

"That's understandable, Jasper. He's your only family."

Jasper sat and sipped on the brandy. Everyone else in the room was occupied with their own thoughts. When he finished, he set the glass aside. He looked more composed and leaned forward.

"We need to get ready for the battle to come. The Magician isn't going to wait. He's going to want to hit hard and quell the loyalists. He will want to strike before he thinks the people rally around you, Prince Alair. I'm going back to town to talk to the men who followed Lirin's attackers. How are you feeling, sire?"

"I am feeling fine, Jasper. I still want to be a part of this."

"Would you like to come speak to the people in town? We can take the horses and not be gone long."

Alair set aside the album and stood up taking Rose into his arms and kissing her forehead.

"Yes, I think that's a good idea. I will be back soon, Rose. Don't worry. I am not sick and the ride will do me good. I intend to stop Balik."

He kissed her again and held her close as they made to leave. She didn't want to let him out of her sight but knew that wasn't logical. Amey noticed that her father used the name 'Balik' and not the term 'the Magician.'

"Be safe," she whispered.

Alair and Jasper left the Lodge and went to the stable. The stable boy had two horses saddled and waiting and watched the prince with wide eyes. Alair raised an eyebrow as he looked over at Jasper and laughed.

"Pretty sure I would come, weren't you?"

"I knew you would be angry about all that your cousin has done. I felt sure you'd want to start to set things right."

"You're right about that. Let's get started, then."

They mounted up and rode the short distance to town. The men had returned. Jasper called for a meeting of the townspeople. The biggest building to hold that many people was the dining room in the inn. All the adults and young adults came. The older children stayed home to look after the infants. Everyone looked at Alair with curiosity. No one had seen him for seventeen years or had never seen him because they had been born after he was ensorcelled. If they thought they recognized him from somewhere, they didn't connect him to their Prince. Jasper waited for everyone to settle.

"Today, the campaign to take back our countries started. We fought and captured around two hundred and fifty of the Magician's men. The diversion we created allowed Queen Angeline, her daughter Rose, and granddaughter Amey to enter the palace and free Prince Alair. I'd like all of you to give a hearty welcome to your Prince."

Jasper spread his arm wide indicating Prince Alair at his side. The people were speechless. They looked closer at the thin man beside Jasper and a dawning wonder spread over their faces as they finally recognized him. They all began to speak at once. To get their attention, Jasper started the cheer.

"Hip hip hurray, Hip hip hurray!"

The cheer went on until the prince held up his hands and called for quiet.

"Thank you, ladies and gentlemen. I am happy to be back. It pains me to think how you have suffered all these years at the hands of my cousin. I have suffered also. I have learned that Balik is responsible for the deaths of my parents. You can be assured I will avenge them. But he has taken more from me than my parents. He has taken my family. He drove away my wife and caused me to think she had deceived and plotted against me. He has deprived me of knowing my daughter. Until today, I didn't know of her existence. I have had seventeen years of my life with my family stolen from me. You can also be assured I will avenge that wrong. Will you help me?"

Alair had spoken from the heart and his people responded in kind. There was no artifice just pure emotion. They shouted their eagerness when he finished speaking. The people crowded around him and welcomed him back. Jasper felt elated by their response and knew that this charismatic man would rally all the people to him.

"Ladies and gentlemen, we need to prepare for imminent battle. You are the first to know the prince is free. No one else knows yet. I want to change that. I want runners to go swiftly to other towns and villages and tell them that their prince will fight with them against the Magician. Warn them to be ready. We have very little time. We expect the attack will begin in the morning at first light"

The people in the room were galvanized into action. Several young men volunteered to carry the message to the others. They shyly came before the prince who thanked them for their courage and shook their hands, wishing them well and Godspeed. The prince joined Jasper and the townsfolk to finalize the plans for the coming battle. They estimated the number of men that they could mobilize and divided them into categories. Some had been trained previously to carry arms and would be in the forefront of the battle. These men were eager to fight for what was theirs. For too many years, they had to hold back for fear of causing their neighbours trouble. But no more! Everyone was eager to take part in whatever way they could and the prince welcomed their participation no matter how minor. The plans were completed within the hour and people returned to their homes to spend an anxious night.

"That went well."

Alair was pleased with the results of the meeting. He and Jasper were mounted on their horses and heading back to the Lodge. They had agreed that the Magician wouldn't start so late in the day and were heading to the Lodge to get some rest, or as much as they could anticipating the coming morning. They were sure the battle would begin not long after dawn.

"What do you know of the power of Balik's forces?"

"We estimate he's hired as many as three thousand mercenaries. Whether all of them will want to fight an outright battle is unknown. He has common criminals and thieves in his employ looking for easy money. These are the men we are questioning whether they will fight. He has used mind control to keep them in line but whether he can coerce them to fight isn't known. Some of the men, however, are seasoned fighting men who also get the chance to brutalize the ones who stand up to them. He has given them free rein and they have taken advantage of that by robbing from the people. They are cruel and heartless men. Your cousin has also taken much from the people and the country. There is no love for him in either kingdom."

Alair was silent as they continued to ride.

"When my father was alive, he told me again and again, 'We only rule the people by the grace of the people.' Where will we meet Balik tomorrow?"

Jasper considered the information he'd heard from the men who followed Lirin's attackers. They had trailed them back to an encampment in the field on the outskirts of the town. They had pitched their tents close up to the edge of the woods less than five miles away. The main population centers were in close striking distance from their campsite.

"I believe if we go to the field beyond the town tomorrow, we will meet one of the forks of his attack. This will not be a conventional battle. There isn't actually an army to fight. His men are not that organized, not even the mercenaries. They are set up as troop commanders but the men under them are not used to organized fighting and have little discipline. Whether Balik will be fighting with his men remains to be seen. We expect him to stay back and use his powers to affect the battle and maintain his mind control over those who are not so willing."

"If that is the case, what do you think of trying to send a small group behind their lines and make an attempt to capture Balik? It would demoralize his men and might just cause them to abandon him. We cannot hope to withstand a prolonged battle."

Jasper was surprised at the prince's grasp of battle tactics. It was an intriguing idea. A dangerous one, but intriguing nonetheless.

Alair saw his surprise and laughed.

"What did you think that I did growing up? Do you not remember how my father and I would set up the soldiers and hold pitched battles to see who could plan the best means of attack? I remember even you took part in our games."

"Yes, I remember. This is the real thing and I think your idea has merit. He would be protected. He does have some men who possess powers. He also has men who carry otherworld weapons. They can kill at great distances. But, yes, that is definitely a plan to think about. He wouldn't be easy to hold. No matter how despicable, he is a great magician. We would have to somehow render him unconscious."

"It would be a great pleasure!"

Jasper laughed. He liked the way this young man thought.

"I'm sure it would, milord, but we need to proceed carefully. We don't want to lose you after all the work we've done to get you back. Your wife would not be pleased."

It was Alair's turn to laugh at the understatement. Rose had barely let him out of her sight since they had rescued him! They completed their trip to the Lodge in companionable silence.

Chapter Sixteen- Engagement

Everyone was ready in the pre-dawn hours. Everyone who could hold a weapon and wanted to be there were present, whatever the age. Those with actual weaponry were in the forefront. There many hearty men who looked more than capable carrying well cared for swords- more men than Jasper had realized would be there with them. Skilled archers would take up positions that would serve them best. They carried extra quivers of fletched arrows that would keep them supplied while more were being prepared at the back of the lines. There would be no shots taken without a sure target in sight and these men did not miss often. Those on horseback were set to harass the flanks of the enemy and the people chosen as protectors who commanded the power of the stones watched over everyone. All others would keep back from the initial battle and use their makeshift weapons in whatever manner was feasible. Scouts reported back that the Magician's men were ready. The battle was to be on several fronts centering around the neighbouring communities but they knew that the Magician would be with this group in front of them. Able leaders were commanding the other fighters and were set up in a similar way to theirs. Reports came in that it was as they thought. Many of the criminals and opportunists that the Magician had working for him had disappeared into the night. Now they only had to wait for daylight.

Alair and Jasper wore similar hardened leather armour reinforced with thin metal plates and forged helmets that the blacksmith had fashioned for those who had weapons. Their horses also sported the hardened leather on head, shins, and flanks. No one had been able to convince Lirin that he should stay behind because of his wounds. There was no way that he would sit this out. Angeline had tended to his bruises so that he wouldn't be hindered in his movement. He also wore the reinforced leather armour and carried a sword, a short bow with a full quiver on his back, and a long-bladed knife at his hip. Angeline,

Rose, and Amey had elected to stay where their talents could be used to help the injured. The older girls had removed the children to a safe place away from the battle while their mothers worked behind the lines to support their men.

Streaks of dawn lightened the sky. Tension was building in anticipation of the coming battle. In the distance, you could hear the sounds of the approaching men. All the men checked their weapons and shifted restlessly. Alair's voice rang out over the stillness.

"Remember this, friends. This is our country and no one will be allowed to take it from us. We will fight and we will win against evil. Today we are fighting to make this land safe for our children. We will show them what we are made of and they will rue the day that they sought to destroy us. God help and protect us all."

The enemy was in sight. You could see the Magician's men arrayed in a three-prong strike formation advancing on the neighbouring communities at the same time. There was a double rank of men marching on the citizens. Townsfolk and farmers were ready to fight side by side for what was theirs and the prince was going to fight with them. They would not let him or their families down.

Jasper stayed with the prince. He would erect a protective barrier to shield them and others fighting around them and hoped to hold out against the onslaught. Lirin was with others to use his power in the same way. They had many more able practitioners spread among the men to protect them as well as they could. All was in readiness.

The first of the enemy were engaged with the swordsmen and both sides fought ferociously. The archers chose their targets to best assist their men. The enemy wasn't advancing easily against these committed citizens. They were met and faced down in a toe-to-toe battle. The townsfolk and farmers fought with a passion that surprised the Magician's men. They were aggressive and indomitable. The defensive wall held and the attackers drew back to regroup for a second offensive.

The wounded were treated and, unless they were unconscious, insisted on going back to the fight.

As the second offensive was launched, Alair turned to Jasper and his look asked the question. Jasper knew what he meant and nodded his head 'yes.' He called on a talented young man to take his place to protect those around him. He and the prince wheeled their horses and Jasper nodded to the small group of men he had chosen for this detail and they all headed for the woods. No one marked their departure except Amey. She wondered what they were doing and watched as they entered the woods turning their mounts toward the position of the Magician's camp. Now she thought she knew. She looked around and saw a horse picketed by the fence. Her mother was tending the wounded and grandmother was nowhere to be seen. Easing away from the other women, she hurried to the horse. There was no saddle but there was a bridle and Amey drew up the reins easing the horse away and headed for the woods to follow. She wasn't sure what she was doing but she just knew she had to go with Jasper and her father.

Amey could see the slight trail the passing horses had made. She followed but at a distance that wouldn't alert them to her presence.

Alair and Jasper approached the Magician's camp and checked out the setup. The Magician stood watching the battle in the distance with his two men standing guard. He hadn't noticed their arrival. Jasper sent their men ahead to skirt the camp and set up around where they would enter. They were to remain out of sight unless Jasper and Alair were threatened.

"We will go in and confront the Magician. His men will only act on his orders. If they should attack us, take care of them."

Surprisingly, Amey found that the Magician's camp wasn't very far to go and she soon came to where the other horses were tied. She tied hers with them and followed the two men into the Magician's camp. It was empty of soldiers but she could hear voices from a short distance away. She crept up to the back of a pitched tent and peered around the corner. There, not ten feet away, stood the Magician with two armed men facing her father and Jasper. She could hear them clearly. The Magician sneered at the prince and said,

"How very foolish of you, Alair. You should've taken advantage of your freedom and gone far away. Both kingdoms are mine now. You are too weak and easily led to be in power here."

"I could not leave until I avenge my parents' deaths, the deaths you arranged. You have made a grave mistake, Balik. You didn't kill me when you had me in your control."

"I have you in my control still, in case you haven't noticed. My men will kill you and your friend here and no one will be the wiser."

Amey realized that the Magician didn't know Jasper. That meant he didn't know he had the power to protect her father from harm. She had to do something to even the sides. The air was still and you could hear the battle in the distance. Perhaps she could make them think there were others coming through the woods. Amey brought out her Bear Claw crystal, concentrated on the stone and sought the power within. The stone seemed alive in her hand and she felt the Light building.

She had moved leaves and pebbles before when Jasper was training her but this would be more involved. She focused on the woods and sent out her thoughts to the trees. She pictured what she wanted to do and sought to rustle the leaves slightly. There was the faintest movement from her efforts. She grasped her crystal tightly and sought her power. She was filled with the Light. She felt it grow in her and sent out her thoughts again. This time the leaves rustled as if a breeze was blowing or someone was brushing past the trees. The men with the Magician turned to look at the spot to see who was there. Amey concentrated on the twigs on the ground. With her mind, she sought to break one. She focused her power and was pleased to hear a twig snap. Again, the men looked.

"Go see who's there," ordered the Magician.

Weapons drawn, the men went toward the trees and Amey again snapped a twig, but a little farther away. The men slowly went in the direction of the sound. As they walked in under the trees, Amey was surprised to hear a muffled grunt and the 'thump' of someone falling. One man was down and the other was turning to run. He too went down. This time, Amey saw a branch the size of her arm continue its swing over his head. Out of the woods stepped her Grandmother Angeline. She didn't look Amey's way although Amey was sure she knew she was there. Instead, she walked across the ground until she was facing the Magician. She spoke with contempt.

"Your men are indisposed. You can expect no help from them. At last, we meet, Magician. It's time you paid for your evil ways."

Sure of himself and his power, Balik was relaxed and unafraid and taunted the queen.

"You overestimate your ability, woman. You have no power to win against me. I can dispose of all of you in an instant, if I wish."

Amey saw her father reach for the pendant that she had made for him. He was seeking the strength of the stones she had assembled. The Magician must be trying to affect his mind. Amey sought her power again and called for the Light. She grasped her crystal and the amulet in her right hand and extended her left toward the Magician. She projected her thoughts and intercepted those the Magician was using to attack her father. She turned them back on Balik and watched with pleasure the surprise spread over his face. He looked quickly to Angeline, suspecting it was she who was deflecting his power. This surprised him. His dominance had never been bested before and he began to feel a sense of unease. Perhaps he had underestimated her. Now his mind turned to escaping. But first, he had to distract them from his intention. Before he could do anything, Angeline spoke.

"You have no chance to rule here now that the prince is back among his people. They will fight for him. Can't you hear? Listen to the sounds of their loyalty. You are finished here."

The Magician had used the time Angeline was speaking to marshal his power and set the stage for his escape. He ordered the elements to allow him to travel to another place. Before he escaped, he spoke to divert their attention from his plan. He spoke with disdain.

"You will lose! You will lose everything and, in the end, it will be I who will have the last laugh. Remember that!"

And he disappeared. Angeline knew what had happened and so did Amey and Jasper. She should have used a containment spell to prevent it. Alair was looking around in shock.

"Where is he? Where has he gone?"

"He has traveled to another plane, I believe. He is no longer here in Freo. He has escaped us. Listen, can you hear the change in the sound of the battle?"

Jasper was right. The battle sounds were dying away while a triumphant roar grew. They were all anxious to get back. Jasper's men came out to join them. Amey stepped from behind the tent putting her crystal in her pocket and went to her father.

"What are you doing here? How did you get here?" Alair was both confused and a little angry. "You could've been hurt coming here like this."

"So could you have, Father," Amey said as she hugged him close. Alair went to speak again but stopped and just hugged her back.

"Let's get back and see what's happening. I think the Magician's control over his men ended when he escaped. We need to tie up these two and leave them to be collected."

Once the Magician's men were firmly secured by Jasper's men, they were led away towards the town. Angeline led the way to the horses. When they were mounted, she said to no one in particular.

"It seems like everyone had the same idea at the same time- to work behind the scenes and take out the cause of the battle at its roots. You and Jasper sought to neutralize the Magician in a preemptive strike. I knew he had to be removed permanently so as not to threaten our future and Amey wanted to be sure everyone was safe. He's gone for now but I don't think we've seen the end of his evil ways."

When they were on their way to the town, her grandmother eased back to ride with her.

"You scared me when you rustled the leaves and broke the sticks because you were leading them right to where I was hiding. I had to think of a plan on the spot. It worked out, though. You've learned your lessons well."

"I had no idea you were there. I just wanted to get them separated so that I could try to do something. I guess I almost messed up your plans. I'm sorry."

"I didn't have the slightest idea what I was going to do. Your plan was just as good as mine."

Amey laughed, "Or as bad."

Grandmother Angeline laughed too. The two men looked back at them to see what was so funny.

After the Magician's men had turned and run, their fighters and all the others assembled on the battleground had collected their wounded and prisoners and returned to the town. Jasper and the Prince along with the queen and Amey arrived back in the town to a boisterous celebration. There were hundreds of people milling in the streets, laughing and drinking toasts to each other. Their arrival was marked by Rose who hurried over.

"Where did you go? I've been worried sick since I couldn't find any of you anywhere."

Alair dismounted, pulled Rose into his arms and gave her a big kiss in front of the whole crowd who roared their approval.

"We went hunting a rat, my love- a very slippery rat who escaped our trap, unfortunately. What is happening here?"

The mayor, his wife and Lirin came up carrying tankards for them all. Lirin stepped to Amey's side and smiled. Once they were supplied with drink, the mayor roared over the noise of the crowd,

"Your majesty, your people rallied to you. When the runners announced your return to the other villages and towns, everyone dropped what they were doing and hurried to your defense. Just as the second offensive began, hundreds of men fell on the Magician's with force and turned the battle. His men knew they were defeated. Those who could ran from the battleground and disappeared into the woods. We have all the others under guard awaiting your judgment." He turned to the crowd and led the cheer, "Three cheers for the prince. Hip hip, hurray! Hip, hip hurray! Hip hip hurray!"

Their Prince looked at his people with shining eyes and a lump in his throat. He held up his tankard to the crowd and took a drink, toasting them and their courage. He spoke so all could hear.

"Thank you. You overwhelm me. Today is your day. You fought for your country and you won. I will be proud to be able to serve you from this day forward."

Alair turned to Rose and Amey. He slipped his arms through theirs and led them into the crowd to celebrate with their people. Lirin followed. Angeline and Jasper hung back. They clinked their mugs together and celebrated the day's victory in quiet contentment.

Chapter Seventeen – Renewal

The celebration lasted for days. Jasper was obliged to send back to the Lodge for the carriage so that the prince with his wife and daughter, and Queen Angeline could travel around to the surrounding communities to present themselves to the people. Jasper and Lirin rode with them to see to their comforts. Everywhere they went crowds gathered and offered them gifts of gratitude from the little that they had. Prince Alair was humbled. He saw what his cousin had done to these good citizens and his anger simmered. He sent to the city and had the royal storage sheds broken open and the necessary foods and goods distributed to the people. He vowed to them that they would never be so abused again as long as he lived. They were finally able to return to the Lodge where Nanny Pearl clucked over them with concern.

"You'll wear yourselves out and then what good will you be? Sit down and rest while I make you some tea and cakes. Supper won't be ready for a good while yet so you'll just have to make do with a simple tray."

With that, she bustled out and they looked at each other with grins on their faces. No one would dare to tell her that they had been feasted all over the place and weren't actually that hungry anyway. They would just have to put up with it and enjoy her care. They were perfectly willing to sit quietly around the livingroom and relax. She returned with a loaded tray and left them to see to the feast.

Amey watched her parents. To tell the truth, she hadn't been able to take her eyes off them for the whole tour around the countryside. She couldn't get over the change in her mother! There was a vibrancy about her that had never been there before. Her mother had always been somewhat withdrawn, encouraging her to go off with her grandmother. She would sometimes accompany them and they would have great fun but she preferred to sit at home reading or writing. Of course, Amey now understood that she had been preoccupied with telling Amey of her background history and writing it all down so that she would understand. But it was something more than that. She now seemed whole- a more rounded personality- as if having her husband back completed her. Amey had never had a father to feel his absence so she didn't find anything different other than the pleasure of actually having a father. She hadn't felt an emptiness in herself that needed filling. Having a father now was a little strange but in a pleasant way. Other than Jasper, she hadn't spent much time around older men. She loved her mother but didn't really know her father yet. What she knew of him she admired and she thought him to be very handsome. On their tour around the countryside, her father revealed a loving and caring nature, a quiet humour and easy manner. He was an easy person to get to know. She caught him looking at her with a dazed look in his eyes from time to time that would melt into a gentle smile when she looked at him. She loved to see the bond between her mother and father and how carefree her mother now seemed. She looked to be settled and content although he had to stop her from fussing.

Amey realized, however, that she was anxious to go home to the farm. Now that all the excitement had died down and she was not under such tremendous pressure, Amey wanted to go back to what was familiar. She didn't consider this to be home and couldn't imagine living in the palace! Home was the white wooden farmhouse at the foot of Bear Claw Mountain in the Grenian Valley. Amey wanted to go home, go back, finish her school year, and get back to some semblance of normal but she didn't know what was to happen now. Her parents were making plans, each one completing the other's sentences as they mapped out their future- a future that included her.

Grandmother Angeline was standing at the window. A warm smile wreathed her face as she watched her daughter and son-in-law in animated conversation and listened to their plans. They had shifted so quickly back to the way they were before as if the intervening years had never happened. After a while, she shifted her gaze to the view outside the window. There was still a faint smile on her face but she was lost in thought. Nanny Pearl bursting through the door drew her attention away from the window.

"Dinner is served. Now, don't delay or it will get cold. After all this excitement, you need to keep up your strength. Lord knows how busy you are going to be from now on."

Nanny Pearl herded them out into the dining room where they stared in amazement at the meal set out before them. The candlelit table groaned under the weight of the glistening, golden turkey with walnut stuffing, the fluffy mounds of mashed potatoes and gravy, and the bowls and bowls of various vegetables. There were baskets of piping hot buns and jewel-like chunks of cranberry jelly.

They looked in consternation at each other and wondered how they were going to do the meal justice and not insult Nanny Pearl who had obviously been working at a manic pace to put this abundance on the table. Squaring their shoulders, they took their places and determined to enjoy the meal ahead.

"Nanny Pearl, you have outdone yourself!" Grandmother exclaimed. Everyone else agreed.

The old woman beamed with pleasure as she served up generous portions to each of them. She bustled back to the kitchen, saying over her shoulder, to the inward groans of the diners,

"You just enjoy that meal there and I will go and get the dessert ready."

When those assembled at the table were settled, Alair lifted his wine glass and waited while the others picked up theirs before he spoke the toast,

"To good food, the company of family and true friends and to peace and prosperity from this day forward."

The meal proved to be excellent and they surprised themselves at the amount of food they ate. They were even able to enjoy the hot apple pie and whipped cream that followed. They had no problem sleeping that night.

Amey awoke to bright sunshine the next morning and the sound of birds singing outside her window. She slept in a smaller room now decorated with pale mauve walls and white lace curtains. The lavender-scented bedding and full stomach from the amazing dinner the night before had made falling asleep easy. Amey lay there enjoying the peacefulness and warmth after the trying days of the last couple of weeks. There was nothing pressing that urged her to rise but she threw aside the covers and got up anyway. She dressed quickly and hurried down the stairs wanting to go for a walk in the peace and quiet of the new day. She stood in the doorway of the patio and breathed in the resinous scent of the nearby pines and cedars. The sun had not yet heated up the day and the cool air was refreshing. Intending to go through the patio to the path that led through the garden, Amey was surprised to find she was not alone. Her Father was sitting on the low railing looking out at the mountains and forest. He was dressed casually in tan pants and an open-necked blue shirt that complimented the dark hair so like her own. He turned his head at her approach.

"Good morning, Amey. You're up early."

"Good morning, Father. So are you. I would've expected you to still be sleeping."

A grin spread across his face and he replied,

"Your Mother is the one who likes to sleep 'til noon. I prefer to get up and enjoy the peace and quiet before the day begins."

Amey was intrigued with this similarity in their natures.

"So do I. I was going for a walk through the garden. Would you like to join me?"

A slow smile spread across his face and he rose gracefully in answer. They stepped off the patio and walked at a leisurely pace in companionable silence towards the garden. The pungent scents of the herbs in the kitchen garden filled the air as they brushed by them. They walked by the newly planted vegetable beds and could smell the rich, earthy scent from the tilled soil. Alair reached out to hold aside the hanging rose branch that had escaped the arbour and they walked on to the end of the garden to where the rustic chairs sat under the overhanging willow. The fresh, new leaves glowed in the early morning light. Alair dusted off the seat of one chair for Amey and they both sat to look back at the peaceful garden. A robin landed on one of the pea poles with its mouth full of dried grass for its nest. After it was sure it was safe, it continued on to the eaves of the shed where it was building its nest. Amey wanted to tell her father about wanting to return to school but didn't know how to broach the subject.

"What troubling you, Amey?"

Amey swung her head around to look in surprise at her father.

"You have a very expressive face," he said and smiled gently in answer to her questioning look. "Is it something that you can talk to me about? I know you haven't had time to get to know me yet but I assure you that I am a good listener."

Amey looked down at her hands in her lap and tried to decide how to broach the subject of her returning to school. She didn't want to hurt her father's feelings- didn't want him to think she didn't want to be with him and her mother. Finally, she decided to just tell him what she thought and see what came of it. She looked into her father's eyes and said,

"I don't want you to get the wrong impression. I am so happy that we have you back but it has been a very unsettling time for me. Until two weeks ago, I didn't know that you existed. Oh, I knew that I had a father, but I was told he had died before I was born. In a short period of time, I found out that you were alive, that I had powers that I didn't know about and that I was expected to use those powers to rescue you. I have travelled from the only home I have ever known to another world and, when we got here, everything has gone too fast. Instead of being just an ordinary girl, I find I am the daughter and granddaughter of royalty. Everything is so strange. Wonderful too! But I just want to go back to the way I was before, go back to school and finish out the year. I want to explore the woods and the mountains around the farm. I want..."

Amey fell silent. She had let it all pour out and now she didn't know how her father was going to take her words. She finally steeled herself to look at him. He wasn't watching her but gazing out at the garden before them.

"Amey, you can understand that I am anxious to get to know you. Your Mother and I have been making plans but I now realize that we haven't included you in the plans nor have we asked your opinion. You are a mature young lady and I am proud of you beyond words. I too have had a surprising time this last little while. There has also been a lot for me to adjust to in the last couple of weeks. I find that I have a full-grown daughter about whom I knew nothing. I have my beloved wife returned to me after I was told she had run away from me. I find that the cousin I trusted killed my parents and then tried to do the same to your mother and grandmother. I see what he has done to my people. It has been a trying period for me also but a happy one."

He turned to look at his daughter. His gaze roamed over her face and hair and he smiled.

"I now have a beautiful daughter who is smart and brave and I have my family back together. I am being a little selfish in wanting to keep you by my side but I can see your point of view. How long before the end of the school year?"

Amey swallowed the lump in her throat and answered.

"There is two months left before summer holidays begin."

"Alright. Let me think on this matter and talk to your mother. We will have the summer to get together. Perhaps I could come to the farm and go on those hikes with you. I promise that we will consider your wishes. Is that alright with you?" Amey nodded, unable to speak.

"Good, then let's go in and see if Nanny Pearl has any coffee or tea ready. I'm not sure that I could eat anything after last night but I could use something hot to drink. How about you?"

Amey gave her father a happy smile and said,

"Yes, I believe a cup of tea would be just perfect now."

He held out his hand to her and Amey placed hers into his. He pulled her to her feet and wrapped his arms around her, giving her a quick hug, one that she returned. Arm in arm they walked slowly back to the Lodge talking easily, sharing stories.

Chapter Eighteen- Interlude

Alair was true to his promise. After breakfast, he and Rose saddled their horses and rode off carrying a picnic basket that Nanny Pearl had hastily packed. They were followed at a discreet distance by mounted guards. Jasper was taking no chance that there weren't any of Balik's supporters or even Balik himself still somewhere around. They had several scouting parties searching the countryside for any remnant of his forces to ensure everyone's safety.

Amey watched them then walked back into the house before going to the living room to get a book to read. Grandmother Angeline stood by the window as she had the night before having obviously watched the departure just as Amey had. She turned as Amey entered and said,

"They'll have a lovely day for a ride." She turned away from the window and sat down on the sofa, patting the seat beside her for Amey to come sit beside her.

"Now, you and I can talk. What's troubling you, dear?"

Amey wasn't surprised that her grandmother had been able to see something was troubling her. She had never been able to hide anything from her since her early childhood. When she was small, she had always thought her grandmother could read her mind. Now she knew that it was because her grandmother understood her so well although, after all she's learned, mind reading wasn't so farfetched. It didn't help either that her face was such an open book.

"I went for a walk with my father in the garden this morning. He also asked me what is wrong and I just poured it all out on him! He is so easy to talk to and I ended up telling him that I wanted to go back to the farm and finish out the school year. We had a good talk and he said that he understood. He said he would talk to Mother for me. I was worried that he would be insulted that I wanted to leave after just finding him again but he really understood. He said that he would like to come to the farm and go hiking with me into the mountains. Do you think I'm being selfish, Grandmother?"

"No, dear, not selfish. You have been through a lot in the last couple of weeks. I'm not surprised that, once everything calmed down, you would try to get back to normal.

Your Father is a remarkable man, Amey, with the ability to relate to people on many levels. It isn't surprising that he would be able to understand his own daughter despite having just met her. You are like him in many ways, you know. You are both aware of everything around you and relate. He will be such a good leader because he understands people's circumstances and feels empathy for them. But he doesn't just care, he tries to solve any problem or situation.

He is a patient man, Amey, and can wait to spend quality time getting to know you, as he wants. He realizes that he, too, will be busy in the next few months getting the kingdom back in order. The Magician has left it in a very bad state and he and your mother have a lot of work to do to repair the damage and get to know each other again. I think you returning to school is an excellent idea. Don't worry, Amey. I think things will work out in the end."

Over the next few days, Prince Alair talked to his wife both in private and with Grandmother Angeline. Jasper was included in these discussions and Amey was consulted also. Plans were being made for the coming weeks and months. Rose was tearful at the thought of not having Amey with them. She had expected everything to follow the wonderful image she had in her mind of a family gathered in a loving home eating meals together and celebrating all the special occasions that they had missed in the past years. Amey assured her that she wanted to be together as a family but that she needed to complete her school year and have some time to adjust. Rose did understand just how unsettling recent events had been for Amey but she was still disappointed. Alair assured her that she would have her family and all the special celebrations that she could want in the future.

Grandmother Angeline surprised everyone when she announced that she wanted to return to the farm also.

"Consider it semi-retirement. The intervening years have been a trying time for me also and I look forward to relaxing and maybe getting to travel and be a tourist. When you and Alair married, Rose, it had been my intention for you to rule both Altidio and Freo. Being the only son of the dead queen and king, Alair would have been crowned king long ago. The Magician made sure that didn't happen. Now that you are together, Alair will no longer be a prince but the king and you his queen- a joining of both kingdoms. Before we escaped to the other world, I had intended to leave the palace for a more secluded lodging. Now that we have the farm, I intend to go there. It is as close as anything I would've chosen earlier. I can be there for Amey and we can travel back and forth whenever it pleases us. You and Alair need to get to know each other again and start to rebuild your life and your kingdoms. You can have the honeymoon that was interrupted."

Jasper spoke up when Angeline finished.

"I will go to the farm also to help out. The Lodge is well run and doesn't need me here. There are many talented people to do the teaching. We have been planning and fighting for a long time and I look forward to a time of peace. I'm getting too old for this sort of thing."

Alair laughed.

"I doubt that your age has much to do with it. You are certainly not old! I would have a hard time keeping up with you but I understand your wish to unwind from all the intrigue and chaos. I reserve the right, however, to call on you when I need you. Agreed?"

"Yes, your majesty. I agree. I would be honoured to serve you whenever I am needed."

Once it was decided, arrangements were made, baggage packed and plans for the summer vacation were formulated. Nanny Pearl planned a going away party and prepared a sumptuous dinner that left everyone feeling content. The villagers also held a reception so that everyone could wish their queen a fitting farewell. They were thankful for her efforts on their behalf in the fight against the Magician but they also felt close to her for her personal care of everyone who needed her help.

The celebrating finally wound down and Amey could see that her mother was putting on a brave face. She went to her when there was a break in the action and she put her arm around her shoulder and said,

"It won't be long till summer, you know. You can now begin to live again. I think I understand you a little better now that I have met my father. Even though you loved me all my life, you grieved the loss of your husband and I reminded you of him every time that you looked at me. Now you have him back and there is a new light in you. You don't want me to go but you know I will be back soon. You will be so busy getting the kingdom back in order that the time will fly. Just pretend it's as it was back on the farm when I went to school. I'll be back before you miss me."

Rose put her head on her daughter's shoulder.

"I didn't dare to plan for the future because I knew that the chances weren't good that we could get him back. When we rescued your father, I finally did dare to dream of having us all together all the time. I guess I didn't acknowledge that you were no longer a child but a young lady. In one more year, you will be finished high school and going off to university and make your way in the world. It's hard to have to adjust my dreams to reality. I know it won't be long until summer and we can spend it becoming the family I see in my dreams."

Amey said,

"We are that family already. We have all the years ahead of us to be the family of your dreams"

Rose straightened up and placed her palms on each side of Amey's face. She looked into her eyes and let her gaze wander over her features.

"I am so happy to have such a lovely, talented daughter and to have your father back that I feel that I will burst with joy. Don't worry, I realize it is for the best that you go back and finish school. Your father will be extremely busy trying to undo all the damage his cousin left behind. We have a lot to do just to get the palace back in shape! I will use this time to clear everything away so that we will have the time free. I am already making plans for the summer. We're going to have a wonderful family holiday!"

Amey hugged her mother close and they continued the preparations in companionable silence.

Chapter Nineteen - Home Again

The day of their departure dawned bright and warm. Nanny Pearl had tried to load them down with all sorts of goodies but they wouldn't have been able to carry them. They filled their packs with some of it and thanked her for her care. Amey kissed her rosy cheeks and had her all flustered and close to tears.

"You take care of yourself, young lady, and come back soon so that I have all my chicks where I can fuss over them."

Lirin was helping to carry their belongings to the glade. Rose and Alair decided it would be better if they didn't go with them and would say their goodbyes at the Lodge. Although Rose was determined not to cry, she did have tears glistening in her eyes. She didn't trust herself to speak. She held Amey for a long time and only released her when Alair took her place.

"I am looking forward to visiting you at the farm so you can fill me in on everything you did growing up. We will explore and you can show me everything and every place you love. I can't wait to see all the wonders of the world where you grew up. Your Mother has me intrigued with the technical advancements there and I want to see them firsthand. Maybe we can introduce some of the advancements here. You'll be my guide. The time will fly by and we will all be together again. Take care of yourself. I want nothing to happen to my new-found daughter."

He kissed her on the cheek and Amey felt an immense surge of emotion. She threw her arms around his neck and kissed him back. Tears shimmered in both sets of remarkable eyes and they smiled through them. Rose put her arms around both of them in silence.

"I love you, Father. Take good care of my mother. Summer will not be here soon enough!"

Her parents stood on the porch and waved until the small group was out of sight. Grandmother Angeline walked beside Amey as they followed the well-trod path through the fragrant woods. It was a beautiful morning and the birds were singing in the trees. They travelled at a leisurely pace, far different from the first trip. Lirin and Jasper were just ahead and were talking as they walked. Amey noticed how the sun shining through the trees turned his hair to gleaming gold. Today he was dressed in a dark brown woodsman shirt over darker brown pants. He had Grandmother Angeline's pack over his shoulders as well as a small one of his own. His bow and quiver were nestled between the two. He walked with an easy grace making no sound on the path. Jasper has a stout walking staff in his hands and had a more relaxed air about him than Amey had seen in quite a long time. In fact, they were all relaxed and enjoying their walk.

They soon reached the glade. Angeline led Jasper away from the two young people to give them a chance to say their goodbyes. She had noticed that Lirin suddenly appeared nervous. She hid a smile.

"Amey, Jasper and I are going to go on ahead. There's no need to hurry. Say goodbye to Lirin and we'll see you at the farm."

Jasper didn't seem to understand but Angeline took his arm and led him to the center of the glade. The peace of the place settled over everything and Angeline and Jasper disappeared.

"I guess it's time for you to go." Lirin looked down at his feet and then up to Amey's face. "It has been great to have you here despite the circumstances. If you don't mind, I'd love to come to the farm sometime. I'd like to see more of your world and all the wonderful things there. I think we could develop some of the advancements here without making all the mistakes your world has made."

Amey's eyes lit up with a smile.

"I'd love you to come. I could take you around and show you everything you want to see. I want to show you Bear Claw Mountain in my dimension. You'll be amazed how alike they are! I get out of school in two months. When can you come?"

Lirin was relieved. He hadn't been sure how she would react to his wish to visit. Now he would look forward to the summer and being able to spend more time with Amey. He smiled and said,

"You let me know when and I will be there. Jasper said I might be able to study there but I don't know how that would work. We'll have to see. I'll miss you."

Amey didn't know what to say but she felt a warm glow at his words.

'I'll miss you too."

A comfortable silence settled on the glade again. Amey didn't want to leave but knew that she had better go.

"Take care of yourself, Lirin. I'll see you this summer."

He hesitated then made up his mind. He leaned forward and kissed Amey.

"You take care of yourself also. I look forward to seeing you again soon."

Amey smiled then hugged him and kissed his cheek. He smelled of the woods and she knew that she would think of him whenever she smelled that fragrance. She squeezed his hand then walked to the center of the glade. She turned to face him and then said,

"Goodbye 'til summer, Lirin. I'll miss you."

She closed her eyes and invoked the prayer. Moments later Lirin was alone in the glade with a lingering smile on his face. He stood there for a while longer then set off to return to the Lodge. The woods were warming rapidly and Lirin enjoyed the peace of the place. He continued in silence thinking of the coming summer. He hadn't gone very far when he heard a discordant noise. He stopped to listen more closely. Coming from a forest path that joined the one he was travelling came the angry muttering of some unidentified man. Lirin didn't know why it made him uneasy but he removed his bow and pulled an arrow free of his quiver. Holding them ready at his side, Lirin waited for the man to enter his path. As he neared, Lirin could make out some of the mutterings and felt a shiver of fear when he heard the word 'magician.' He pulled back on the bow and aimed where the man would appear.

"Halt," he commanded when the man appeared. He recognized him immediately as one of the magician's men who had set upon him in the village. The man stopped in shock and threw up his hands. He was well armed with knife, cudgel and a staff equipped with a spearhead.

"I know you. You're one of the Magician's men. What are you doing here?" he asked.

"None of your business. I have every right to be on this path."

The scruffy man tried for bravado but fell far short.

"We'll just take you to the king and see what he has to say. Turn around."

Lirin had a length of rope in one of his pocket and he used it to tie the man's hands behind his back. He removed a wicked-looking knife from his prisoner's belt, attaching it to his own and then hung the cudgel by its thong on his pack. He stood the staff against a tree. He turned him around again and looked closely into his face. He had to find out why he was there.

"Where is your master? I heard you mumbling his name as you came along the path. I ask you again, what are you doing here?"

His prisoner looked at him but didn't speak. Lirin removed his own knife from his belt and held it up for the scoundrel to see.

"I have unfinished business with you. I didn't get a chance last time we met. I have no reason to treat you with care so you might find it wise to answer me."

The man looked at the knife with fear. Like all bullies, he was a coward. He looked into Lirin's eyes and read no mercy there.

"Alright, I'll tell you. The Magician just turned me loose without so much as thank you. He said he didn't need me, just the two men he always has with him. He said he couldn't pay me just now but he'd be back soon and wanted me to wait. He must be crazy to think that I'd wait around for him. Fat chance he'd come back and pay me."

"Where was he going?"

Lirin was afraid he knew but wanted to have it confirmed. He felt a chill that went straight to his bones.

"He said that he was going to teach that old woman to mind her own business. He was going to use her to get back into power. He went to the other world to wait for her to go back."

Lirin's fears were realized. The Magician was going to the farm. Everyone there was in danger. They were walking into a trap! He wedged the staff through his prisoner's bonds, securing him to a sturdy sapling and concentrated to send his thoughts to the Lodge, warning them of the danger and telling them to come and get the prisoner and that they'd need help at the farm. He turned and started off at a run to the glade.

"Come back! You can't leave me here like this!"

The voice faded in the distance as Lirin ran back to the glade. He settled his mind and invoked the prayer. He followed Amey, Queen Angeline and Jasper to the other dimension and hoped he wasn't too late.

Angeline and Jasper were in no hurry. The day in this dimension was as lovely as it had been when they had departed the other. As they walked, they discussed what they wanted to do first. Jasper had ideas for the farm that he discussed with Angeline. They made plans to get all the supplies that Amey would need to get back to school. She would need some new books, clothes, and many other things. They would go to town to buy what was necessary.

The walk through the woods was pleasant and Angeline felt as if she were coming home. She realized that, in the years that she had been in exile at the farm, it had become more home to her than Altidio. She certainly enjoyed the freedom she felt here. She had been right to turn over the reins of power to Rose and Alair. They would make worthy caretakers for the people.

The farmhouse came into view through the trees. Everything was calm and peaceful. Heading to the kitchen door, Angeline called over her shoulder to Jasper,

"Come in and I'll make you a tea."

Jasper had slowed his steps as he approached the door. He had a puzzled expression on his face. Entering through the door, Angeline asked what was wrong. Too late did Jasper realize the problem- there was no birdsong! At the same time as this thought entered his mind, an arm snaked out from behind the door and wrapped itself around Angeline's neck. Jasper leapt forward but halted as a knifepoint pressed against her throat. Emerging into full view was the Magician with an evil smile upon his face.

"We meet again. Welcome home. I can see that you didn't expect a welcoming committee. Come in, but carefully."

He eased his way back into the room dragging Angeline with him, the knife kept against her pulse point. Never letting up on the pressure he said,

"Don't try to be a hero. It would be a shame if harm came to this lovely woman. Step carefully into the room and keep your hands where I can see them. My men have gone to get the car and will be back here soon. Move over to that chair and sit down. We might as well be comfortable while we wait."

The Magician led the way into the den. He indicated with a jerk of his head that Jasper move away from the door in the direction of the chair indicated.

"Sit down in that chair and place your hands on the arms." Jasper did as he was told. The Magician forced Angeline over to Jasper and transferred the knife to his neck. He pulled a length of fine, strong rope from his pocket and passed some of it to Angeline.

"You have enough there. Tie his hands to the arms and use the extra to secure his ankles."

Angeline wrapped the rope around Jasper's wrist and the arm of the chair then stretched it over to the other arm hoping to leave a little slack for Jasper to get loose but the Magician was aware of her attempt.

"Pull that tighter. Don't think you can make his bonds loose enough for him to work his way free."

Angeline pulled the rope tighter and looked up into Jasper's face. She could see no solution offered there just a helpless anger. She wracked her brain for ways to turn the tables.

"Now you take the other chair and we will wait." The Magician used the remaining cord to tie Angeline to her chair also then he sat on the settee midway between the two. He checked his wrist watch and Angeline could see that he had purchased it in this dimension. She looked him over carefully and could see that wasn't all he had purchased here. His clothing showed modern tailoring and his shoes were of high quality. She wondered just where he came through the barrier and holed up when he did. She knew that there were other thresholds but hadn't tried them. If they made it out of this alive, she would make sure she explored them all.

Balik looked at his watch again with a scowl on his face. His men seemed to be delayed! She smiled inwardly at his annoyance.

Angeline was leaned back in her chair with an ease that she did not feel. Jasper was looking intently out the window to the patio and wasn't meeting her eyes. She looked over at the man who held them prisoner.

"What do you expect to achieve here," she asked.

"I expect to use you as a bargaining tool to get back my power. I would imagine that your daughter would want to see you safe. Alair will see the wisdom of stepping aside to save your life. He is such a sensitive young man!"

The contempt in his voice showed his opinion of compassion and other such noble feelings.

"I think you are mistaken. What is one person's life compared to the kingdom he has sworn to protect? Any one of us could have been killed during the battle to defeat you. Sometimes one person will die to achieve the freedom for the many. I would not pin my hopes on winning power in that way."

"You'd better hope that I do or your life will be forfeit. I have no problem with the thought of killing both of you if I do not regain power."

"Then where does that leave you ?" Jasper asked "Still out of power where you should be. Do you think that the people would let you back now that they have rid themselves of you?"

The Magician was visibly angered by the question. Angeline couldn't understand what Jasper was trying to do by provoking him.

"They will have no choice. My power will see to it that."

With that, the Magician surged to his feet and stood behind Jasper's chair, tangled his hand in his hair and stretched his head back putting the knife to his neck.

"I could kill you so easily! One flick of my wrist and it is done."

There was madness in his eyes as he contemplated the action. His arm tensed ready to act when a deafening "NO" filled the room

Chapter Twenty - Revenge

Amey arrived at the sun-drenched glade. The familiar, warm fragrance filled her and welcomed her home. She felt like throwing her arms in the air and dancing for joy. She looked up at the mountain, her mountain, rising above and, in her mind, spoke to it.

"I'm back!"

Her gaze took in everything around her. Eventually, she stepped out of the glade and made her way along the path that followed the stream. Amey set aside her pack and sat on the big, flat rock under the willow enjoying the quiet. She could see a long way up the valley and enjoyed the fresh green of the new growth. Leaning over, she scooped the icy water to her mouth and laughed as some dripped down her shirt. The rock was large enough so she lay back on the sun-warmed surface. This was the first time that she had been alone and relaxed for a long time and she enjoyed the experience.

The sun beat down on her and Amey knew that she would fall asleep there if she stayed much longer. Not that there was any reason to hurry. Grandmother knew that she was safe in these woods. She sat up, pulled her pack over to her and removed the package of food that Nanny Pearl insisted she take. There was a big piece of cinnamon cake and Amey leaned back on an elbow to enjoy the treat. She dusted the sugary crumbs from her shirt and scooped another handful of water to her mouth. Time to go. Replacing the food in her pack, she rose in one graceful motion slinging her pack over her back.

The path through the woods was more shaded and the air was redolent with the scent of the evergreens. She strolled at a leisurely pace along the well-marked way watching small squirrels scamper away into the underbrush. She smiled at their furtive ways. What a difference from the last time she had been on this path! Then there had been fear and confusion. So much had happened to her since that time. She had a father! That alone was a momentous thing. Amey needed the semblance of normalcy that being back at the farm would give her. She had many strange things to work out in her mind before summer came.

She was approaching the edge of the woods by the farm when she heard someone coming up fast from behind. She couldn't think who it could be. Amey was astonished to see Lirin come running around the bend in the path. Relief showed on his face as he reached her and took her in his arms, holding her tightly.

"Lirin, what are you doing here?"

Breathless, he said,

"I'm in time," and gradually released Amey from his arms. He fought to regulate his breathing so that he could tell her.

"Amey, after I left you in the glade, I ran across one of the Magician's men, one of the ones who beat me. I surprised him and forced him to tell me what he was doing there. He told me that the Magician had come here to capture your grandmother to use as a hostage to get back into power."

Lirin was still breathing heavily and stopped to get his breath. In the silence that followed, Amey noticed what she had failed to before-there was no birdsong!

"He's here. His evil has silenced the birds just as it did when we had to escape before. He must have captured them by now."

Amey stopped and looked in despair at Lirin.

"What can we do? We have to rescue them!"

Amey tried to think. The happiness had evaporated with Lirin's first words leaving a hollow feeling inside. It still wasn't over! Amey chose action over despair.

"Come on, Lirin. We will approach the farmhouse more carefully. How many are there?"

"The man spoke of only the Magician and his two bodyguards."

"Good, there are four of us. The odds are not too bad. We will approach the house and try to see where they are. Let's try to get a clear view of the windows to find out what we can do. Follow close behind me."

Amey and Lirin skirted the edge of the woods, keeping out of sight but able to see the house. As they rounded the patio, through the glass doors, Amey could see the Magician seated on the settee in front of the window. They could move closer as the trees grew near to the house here. Amey could see Grandmother in the chair to his left and, after moving further, could see Jasper in the chair to his right. She couldn't make out what her grandmother was saying. Jasper turned his head toward the patio and looked out directly at them. He showed no sign of seeing them but Amey knew that he had. Amey felt for a mental connection to Jasper and was rewarded when she felt his thoughts touch her mind.

"The Magician's men will be here soon to take your grandmother away. I will distract him while you create a diversion."

"Jasper, Lirin is here with me. We will free you before they come back."

Amey turned to Lirin and spoke softly in his ear, telling him of Jasper's warning. She saw Jasper turn his head toward the Magician and start to speak. Whatever he was saying enraged the Magician who leapt off the settee. He rushed behind Jasper grasping his hair pulling his head back and holding a knife to his throat. Amey was horrified. She surged forward to the door before Lirin knew what she was doing. She burst into the den with her hand extended and shouted a long drawn out,

"Nooooo!"

The force of her fear for Jasper erupted as an energy that slammed into the Magician and sent him crashing into the wall where, with a stunned look, he slid down unconscious. Amey was astonished that she was responsible for the Magician's condition. She pulled back her hand hiding it against her stomach. For a moment, no one spoke or made a sound then her Amey rushed over to Jasper and freed him while

Lirin freed Angeline. Jasper stood rubbing his wrists looking at Amey in stunned silence. Lirin, however, found his voice and said with awe,

"That was just incredible!"

Amey was still horrified at what had happened and turned her questioning look to her grandmother and asked,

"Grandmother, what did I do?"

Her grandmother took Amey in her arms to soothe her and said against her hair,

"I don't know, dear, but I am happy that you did. He would've killed Jasper."

And to Jasper she said,

"What were you thinking, Jasper? If Amey hadn't been able to strike as she did, you would be dead!"

She turned her attention back to Amey.

"We know some of what the power of the Light can do but you keep showing us how little we really know. Your will to protect found a physical expression and saved Jasper's life. You asked us before whether we needed ritual to work through the stones. Well, apparently you don't. Your reaction was instinctual and the power rushed to answer your call to save Jasper. Your action wasn't to harm but to protect."

Amey turned her head against her grandmother's shoulder to look at the crumpled heap the Magician made on the floor where Jasper and Lirin had gone to secure him before he regained consciousness and said in a small voice,

"Is he dead?"

Lirin went and knelt by the inert body and felt for a pulse. He had used the strong cord that had bound Jasper to secure the Magician's hand and feet. Lirin looked up at Amey and eased her fears.

"He is alive. His pulse is strong."

Some of the tension went out of Amey's body. Jasper broke through her dazed state and addressed the matter at hand.

"We must hurry and make a plan of action before his men return. Lirin has used the Magician's special rope to tie him up but that won't hold him long."

When he stood up, Lirin offered to go out and watch for the two henchmen. Amey needed to get out of the room and said, "I'll come with you," as she hurried to follow.

Jasper and Angeline watched the two young people rush from the room then turned to each other in consternation. Neither knew what to make of the breathtaking display of force they had just witnessed. It was beyond their knowledge of the power of the Light and they didn't know how to guide the young, frightened girl who had escaped from the room as if all the demons of hell were chasing her. They had no time to deal with it now, as they must come up with a plan. Jasper looked to Angeline and asked,

"We have to work quickly. Do we wait for those two men to come and capture them? We have to secure the Magician better than just tying him up. He would make short work of those bonds when he wakes. How does one deal with a powerful magician short of killing him?" he said at a loss on how to proceed.

Angeline didn't answer but was desperately trying to think clearly. How do you control a magician? Certainly, this world had little experience with one so, it made sense that they take the Magician back to be dealt with in the other dimension. Surely, someone there would know what to do with him.

"Can we capture the Magician's two men?" she asked.

"We don't have a lot of time to set something up but I think we can do it. Lirin and I should be able to surprise them. They aren't expecting us to be out here. They believe the Magician will already have captured you and they will just be helping to remove you to their boat. But we need to do something about the Magician. What if he regains consciousness before we have them subdued?"

Angeline thought that she might have an answer to that question. Because Rose had been so worried and preoccupied with the idea of telling Amey of her history, she had been unable to sleep. All the attempts to ease her condition had proved fruitless so Angeline had insisted that Rose go to a doctor and get some medicine to help her sleep. Rose hated to take medicine and there was still a good supply of it in the cabinet in the bathroom. Angeline hurried to find them while telling Jasper of her plan.

"Jasper, you will have to help me with the Magician. Check his pulse again and make sure it is strong. I'm going to dissolve some of Rose's sleeping medicine in water. Can you lift his head so that I can get it into him?"

Angeline read the label for dosage and did a quick calculation according to the Magician's estimated size and crumbled them into the water. Not sure if that would be enough, she added another two to be sure and put the rest into her pocket. She came back stirring the crumbled tablets into a glass of water. Jasper knelt beside the Magician and put an arm around his shoulders to support him. His head dropped back on Jasper's shoulder.

"How much did you put in there?" Jasper asked eyeing the glass warily. "Are you sure this is safe?"

"No, I'm not sure. I don't know what Amey's power has done to him. I read the directions for the medicine and just increased the amount enough so that he should sleep soundly while we take care of his men. I may have to give him more so that we can take him to Freo and turn him over to Alair. I'll put the rest in a water bottle to take with us. There will be someone there who will know how to deal with him."

She knelt in front of the Magician and eased his mouth open. She put the glass to his mouth and poured some of the sleeping draught into his mouth. It was necessary to massage his throat so that the medicine would go down without choking him. It was a slow process.

Finally, when the glass was empty, Jasper eased him back down and arranged him more comfortably.

"I'm going out to the shed to get some strong rope. Those men are returning with the car and need to park behind the house. Lirin and I will hide in the trees on either side of that area and, when they emerge from the car, we'll try to take them there. We have surprise on our side. Unless they come back by themselves, you and Amey might have to deal with the driver."

Jasper quickly left to get the rope. Angeline followed and waited for his return. Together they went to find Lirin and Amey. Lirin turned at their approach and said,

"No sign of them yet."

Jasper hurriedly explained the plan. Lirin ran off toward the patio and came back with the cudgel that had been hanging on his pack. This he handed to Amey who slipped her hand through the thong.

"Don't hesitate to use this if you have to. The driver isn't likely to want his head bashed in and probably won't bother us."

They each took their places. Amey and Grandmother Angeline settled together behind the gnarled trunks of two intertwined trees. Angeline studied her granddaughter's face and saw the fear and uncertainty there. This was yet another step down an unfamiliar path for her granddaughter but Angeline had no way to change anything that might come. She offered what reassurance that she could.

"Amey, everything is going to be alright. None of what has happened is on you. I know you're scared but I want you to know this- you are a good person. A good person only uses her power for good. You saved Jasper's life! I am as stunned as you are about the strength of yours but, I promise you, we will find a master to show you how to control it. He will be able to guide you and make you feel more in touch with your abilities. We will all be there to help you."

Amey continued to stare off into the distance. Angeline took her chin in her hand and turned it towards her.

"I promise you, Amey. You have nothing to fear."

Amey couldn't speak but nodded her head in understanding. Suddenly, they could hear a vehicle coming up the driveway. Angeline squeezed her hand and settled deeper out of sight. She could see Jasper and Lirin do the same. The big, black car drove smoothly into view and made the turn towards the house. Inside were just the same two men that Amey had seen before. She was relieved that she wouldn't have to threaten violence against the driver and could leave the two men to Jasper and Lirin. The car pulled to a stop mere feet away from their position. Saying nothing to each other, the two men opened the doors and stepped out onto the gravel. They didn't look around appearing at ease. As they started for the house, Jasper and Lirin launched at the men from their hiding place and held long knives to their throats.

Angeline rushed forward to take the rope that Jasper held out and proceeded to tie the one man's hands behind his back. Amey was right behind her grandmother but had farther to go to reach Lirin's man. Before she could secure his hands, the big man had shifted and disarmed Lirin. He wrapped his huge hands around Lirin's throat and was squeezing hard. Lirin's face reddened and his hands were unable to break the hold. Amey didn't stop to think. She raised the cudgel and brought it down on the big man's head. His hands freed Lirin and he slumped back against the car. Lirin quickly tied his hands. Lirin looked over at Amey with an embarrassed smile.

"Thanks."

Amey had recovered from her fear and gave Lirin back a small smile.

"You're welcome."

Neither needed to say more. Lirin knew that she had scared herself with the force the power she had used against the Magician and, if he thought about it, he was still in awe of it himself. Amey feared that the power was making her into something evil. Lirin had tried to reassure her that what she did to the Magician wasn't evil but was done to protect Jasper. It was done out of love for him.

"Are you alright, Amey? You were marvellous in there! Thank you for acting so fast to save Jasper. I don't know how you did it but I am just happy that you did. Being able to use your gift to save another is a great thing."

Amey just looked at him solemnly before looking away. He wasn't sure that he'd made her understand but knew it would be best to let it all sink in and let her come to that conclusion by herself.

The man Amey clubbed recovered quickly. They removed all the weapons that they found including two handguns. Jasper and Lirin with Amey and Angeline's help brought the two men into the house. The men were amazed when they saw the Magician out of commission on the floor. Their confidence sagged when they realized that they couldn't depend on him to free them. They wondered how one old man and woman and two young people had overpowered him.

Angeline spoke to Jasper and told him that she was going to contact the Lodge to let them know that they were bringing their prisoners back. Jasper and Lirin discussed how they could carry the Magician to the glade. Each suggested possible strategies and discarded them as unworkable. Amey suggested a native travois. Lirin wasn't familiar with a travois so Amey described it to him.

"It's an ancient form of sled used by native tribes to drag heavy loads. You take two long poles and lash them together at the top then you spread out the bottom ends. You take shorter pieces and attach them to the longer one. It looks kind of like a ladder that's joined at the top. We could lay the Magician on it and drag him to the glade."

"That would work, I think.," Lirin said. "One of us could pull this while the other kept their eye on the prisoners. Amey and I will go out and see what we can put together. Be right back."

"Look in my workroom," said Jasper. " I have some leather strips in there that should work and the hatchet is over by the woodshed."

Jasper directed the two men to sit in the chairs and sat opposite them with a handgun at the ready. Angeline came back into the room and Jasper outlined their plan.

"Good. They will be ready for us in the glade. They have sent for a master who, with other practitioners, will take charge of the Magician and his men. We must go soon."

Amey and Lirin came back in the house with the travois they had rigged up and proceeded to lay it out on the floor by the Magician. Jasper and Lirin lifted him onto the cloth stretched between the poles and secured him with rope so he wouldn't fall out. Lirin took the first turn at the poles and dragged the travois out onto the patio. Jasper directed the two men to follow behind while keeping the gun trained on them at all times. Angeline and Amey followed behind.

It was slow going. The path was a good one for walking but more difficult when pulling a cumbersome device with a full-grown man strapped down on it. Jasper and Lirin took turns. When they finally reached the glade, they were tired. They lay the travois propped against a tree stump and caught their breath before they attempted to cross to the dimension barrier. Amey brought them water from the creek. Perhaps their guard was too relaxed because, suddenly, their two prisoners took off running through the woods. Jasper and Lirin leapt after them. The men were encumbered having their hands tied behind their backs but crashed through the underbrush at a swift pace. Amey and Angeline walked to the edge of the woods and watched. They did not notice the movement on the travois behind them until they were alerted by the brush of the travois slipping against the stump. They whirled around to find themselves face to face with the Magician and a gun. Where did he get a gun?

"Sorry to change your plans, ladies. When they return, I want to discuss your ability to render me unconscious. Now, why don't you sit down there on that log while we wait for my men? Your friends don't stand a chance against them."

Angeline and Amey sat down on a fallen log while he stood hovering over them. They waited in silence.

There had to be something that they could do to get away. Both Amey and Angeline cautiously looked around. They wanted to find something that they could use as a weapon. Angeline moved her hand slowly back so as not to attract attention. There was a decent size rock just behind the log that was shaped to make it easy to grasp. She reached down to test how easy it would be to move. Her fingers grasped the handhold and found it lifted readily at her light tug. Angeline looked at Amey and, with her eyes, directed her attention to the rock. Amey nodded her understanding and looked down. Angeline saw a weathered branch a little bigger than a baseball bat in her hand. She smiled remembering that Amey had been a good player on the school baseball team. She tried to direct what they would do with her eyes not daring to communicate directly to Amey's mind with the Magician so close in case he could sense it. She wanted Amey to take the legs from under the Magician with the tree limb and she would bring the stone down on the Magician's head. They couldn't afford to make any mistake. Angeline's eyes asked the question and Amey gave an imperceptible nod. She tightened her grasp on the wood, eased her arm back to get some leverage and swung the branch. The wood flew with a "whoosh" and caught the Magician behind the knees. He let out a startled cry which was cut off when Angeline leapt up bringing the stone down on his head. He fell for a second time. They didn't wait to see how injured he was. They dropped their improvised weapons and ran off toward the mountain. Despite their flight, Amey remarked to her grandmother in a breathless voice,

"He's going to have some headache after today."

Chapter Twenty-One – Retreat to Bear Claw Mountain

The nervous tension had them both stifling giggles but didn't slow their pace. From behind, they could hear a roar of anger and knew that they hadn't hindered the Magician as much as they hoped. His men must be in sight for the Magician called out to them to follow him. Worry about Jasper and Lirin was in both women's minds. They could now hear crashing in the woods off to their left effectively cutting off their escape route. They would have to climb. They headed for the trail that led to the cave skirting around the slide fan and raced up the path. They looked back in time to see the Magician coming out of the trees. His men were not in sight yet. Amey and Angeline continued to climb. The path soon emerged above the tree line but they didn't stop to enjoy the panorama laid out below them. Amey remembered that, on the other mountain, this path didn't go beyond the cave. She had no idea whether it would be the same here but they would find out soon enough. Up ahead the path curved around an outcropping a short way below the cave. They raced on. They looked back as they rounded the curve and sped on. The Magician's two men were scrambling up over the rock fall and the Magician wasn't far behind them, rounding the outcropping on the path. Amey was relieved to see that the way wasn't blocked beyond the cave. As they drew level with the entrance, an ominous rumble could be heard which grew rapidly in intensity. Angeline and Amey skidded to a stop undecided whether to go on or not. When the rumble turned to a roar, they ducked into the relative security of the cave but didn't venture in too far for fear of falling rock. They hugged the side closest to the tumbling rocks. The sound of the avalanche was deafening and they could feel the concussion right through their bodies. Huge boulders bounced past the entrance. They had to pull their clothing over their mouths to keep out the choking dust. The slide seemed to go on forever. Gradually the noise and motion ended and, were it not for the swirling dust, you would not know anything out of the ordinary had happened. They were covered from head to toe in a coating of fine dust. With relief, they fell into each other's arms and held on tight. Their pulses returned to normal and now they had to decide what to do. Amey voiced her thoughts.

"The Magician's men were on the rock fall when the slide began. Do you think that they were able to get out of the way?"

"I don't know. The Magician had passed the outcropping on the path so he would've been in the open also. He might've had time to will himself to safety. We've seen that before."

They plucked up their courage and stepped out of the cave. The dust was settling so that the sun revealed an amazing scene. Large boulders had crashed into the mountainside and narrowed the path considerably. The rock outcropping was reduced by half and, if the Magician hadn't had time to use his power to remove himself to safety, then he couldn't have survived. There was no sign on the rock fall of the other men. Amey felt sadness at the loss of life despite their evil intentions. It would've been a horrible and frightening way to die. She looked at the rock wall in front of her and put her hand on the sun-warmed surface. She felt a oneness with this mountain. Yet again, she felt that Bear Claw Mountain was watching over her, protecting her. She offered it her thanks.

Shouts from below attracted their attention. They could hear their names being called and were relieved to recognize Jasper and Lirin's voices.

"We're here," they called back. "We're coming down."

They started back down the path and had to be careful on the spots that had been broken away. The sun was hot on their backs and they were grateful when the path entered under the forest canopy. They saw Jasper and Lirin waiting at the foot of the path. Lirin had a nasty gash over his left eye but otherwise appeared uninjured. Jasper didn't have any outward signs of injury but he was moving gingerly. They met and everyone tried to talk at once.

"Are you alright?"

"Are you hurt?"

"Where's the Magician?

"Thank heavens you're safe!"

They also stopped talking at the same time and had to laugh at themselves. Angeline lightly touched the gash on Lirin's head and said,

"You're hurt. Let's get back to the glade where we can wash this out. You have a headache from this wound."

It wasn't a question and Lirin could feel the warmth of her healing touch and felt the pain float away. He smiled his thanks. Jasper looked Angeline and Amey up and down. He rubbed his finger down Amey's cheek and grinned.

"You two are covered in dust. How did you escape the slide?"

Amey looked at her grandmother and down at herself. She brushed her hands over her shirt without much result so gave up the effort.

"We were right beside the cave entrance when we heard the first rumble and were able to just slip inside. The Magician's two men were on the rock fall and I don't know if they were able to get to safety. The Magician was right behind us in front of the rock outcropping. The slide removed half of that rock. There's no sign of him up there. He might've had time to use his magic to escape but we don't know. What happened when you went after those two men?"

Jasper and Lirin looked a little embarrassed.

"We took off after them thinking they wouldn't get far tied up as they were. I should've known better. Obviously, the Magician had loosened their ropes as he did his and, when they appeared to be tiring, we caught up to them and they ambushed us. We were caught unawares and one knocked Lirin out while the other punched me under the chin and in the stomach. I couldn't catch my breath. I suppose we were lucky. They just wanted to get back to help their boss. I'm sorry we weren't more help."

Angeline patted his arm in comfort and said,

"Don't worry, Jasper. We're all safe. That's all that matters."

They returned to the glade and found both Rose and Alair accompanied by a dozen men waiting there.

"Good heavens! What happened to you?"

Rose's worried face relaxed and then broke into a broad smile as she took a closer look.

"I don't think I've ever seen anyone dirtier! What a sight."

She laughed out loud but Alair wanted information. He took in the gash on Lirin's head and the growing bruise on Jasper's swollen jaw. Jasper saw the question on his face and said,

"They got away from us. The Magician pretended to be unconscious. We had his men tied up and had rigged a carrier to bring the Magician to the glade. We got them here but his men created a diversion and we fell for it. When they ran off into the woods, Lirin and I followed."

Angeline took up the tale.

"We watched while they were chasing them, not thinking we needed to keep our eye on the Magician. Apparently, the sleeping pills we gave didn't work on him. We realized too late when he came up behind us. He had us sit on that log until his men got rid of Jasper and Lirin. Amey and I found things to use as weapons. Amey took up a branch and hit him in his legs behind his knees. When he was falling, I hit him in the head with a rock. We didn't wait to see if he was truly injured- we just ran. We could hear his men cutting off our escape and had to take the path to the cave. There was a slide but we were able to shelter in the cave while it passed. I don't know what happened to the others. His men were on the rock fall when the slide came down and the Magician was in a bad place on the path. We don't know what happened to them for sure."

Alair and Rose asked more questions. Rose looked at her daughter with worry when Angeline told them about Amey saving Jasper's life. She understood that this was one more thing for Amey to deal with and determined to talk to her mother. They needed to find a way to help Amey adjust.

Chapter Twenty-Two – Reflection

It was decided that Rose and Alair would come to the farmhouse. Alair directed his men to go back and tell everyone that they would return in a day or two. He, too, knew that Amey would be in turmoil over this new manifestation of her power and wanted to comfort her however he could. He admitted that he was also curious to see the differences here in this world.

The farmhouse was welcoming. After all the excitement, they found that they were hungry. Angeline and Rose went to the kitchen to see what there was to eat. Amey sat in the window seat and looked out at the fields beyond. She was lost in thought and, when Lirin came to sit at the other end of the seat, she turned her troubled eyes to him. It wasn't hard to see what was on her mind.

"Lirin, what is happening to me? I could've killed him! I didn't try to do anything. I didn't even think! All I wanted was to distract him from killing Jasper."

The misery showing on her face was evident in her voice. Lirin had no answer to her question. He had never seen the Light used the way Amey could. He knew, however, that her use of the power wasn't done with evil intentions. She had defended Jasper and prevented his death but he knew that Amey wasn't thinking about that aspect of her action. He needed to reassure her and carefully formulated his answer.

"Amey, I know you're worried about the way you can use the power of the Light. I can't say that I understand it any more than you do, but I know you. You are good and loving and, what you did wasn't to cause injury it was to prevent it. I think that the power was as strong as it was because of your fear for Jasper. You knew something had to be done quickly and you did it without thinking. I have been taught from the time I was small in the use of the power. You can't expect to know everything you need to know in such a short time."

He put a comforting hand over hers.

"We will find a way to teach you to control it. There are brilliant people who can help you. Try to remember that the power of the Light is good and so are you."

Lirin was glad to see some of the self-doubt leave her eyes. She offered him a slight smile and thanked him. Her mother came up with cups of steaming tea for them. She ran her hand gently over Amey's head and, when Amey looked up at her, quietly asked,

"Are you alright?"

Amey smiled and assured her that she was.

"Lirin has been talking to me. I was scared with what happened."

"I know, Amey. Your grandmother and I have been talking about ways to help you. Jasper reminded us of a man who lives alone in the mountains who is a master in the power of the Light. He lives as a hermit and I haven't seen him since I was a little girl. Jasper told us that he is still alive although he is very old. We are hoping that we can ask him to help you. When your father and I return to Freo, we will find him. Try not to worry."

The mood in the room lightened and everyone was able to relax and enjoy the food that was found. Alair was fascinated by everything in the house. While the women were putting together a meal, Alair was twisting knobs, pushing buttons, and asking all kinds of questions. His childlike curiosity made the others look at their everyday articles in a different way. He asked questions about the electricity and how it was made. He wanted to know what the material was that the squeezable bottles were made from. He was fascinated by the phone, the television and couldn't believe that the music came from the small box on the shelf when Amey turned on the CD player. He went outside to look at the car that the Magician's men had left behind and marveled when Rose took him for a short ride in their jeep. He asked all kinds of questions about the vehicle and soon exhausted their knowledge. He realized that he would need more time in this world to explore all the advancements. He could imagine introducing all these wonder for his people. Angeline ventured to caution him.

"You know, Alair, not all the conveniences in this world have come about without harm to the environment and to the community at large. Some of the everyday scientific discoveries have caused pollution of the air and water. I wanted to bring some of these things back for the people but decided to take it very slowly so that we don't make the same mistakes that they have here. There are definitely some small things that can be done right now that would improve the lives of the people."

Alair nodded his head at her warning and determined that he would have to get all the knowledge that he would need to make sound decisions. When he mentioned that he wanted to get as much information as possible, Amey took him over to the desk and turned on the computer. All Alair could do was shake his head with amazement. He watched in fascination as she typed in the search questions and found the needed information. She printed off several pages and handed them to him after only a few minutes. He looked at them strangely then up to Amey's face. He suddenly burst out laughing at the wonder of it all. Amey couldn't help but join in. Alair merrily wrapped her in his arms while the others looked on with knowing smiles. He pulled up a chair and sat beside her.

"This is amazing, simply amazing!"

Amey and Alair continued their searches and the pages piled up. The evening passed quietly and the stress of the day gradually left them. Plans were made for the next day.

"I think we should continue with our original plan, Jasper. We'll go to town and get all the things Amey needs for school. We can't let our uncertainty about the Magician's fate interfere."

Angeline looked over at Alair with a twinkle in her eye and asked,

"Is it safe to take you with us?"

Alair laughed and promised to control himself. He was looking forward to seeing as much as he could in the short time he was there. He was already looking forward to the summer.

The next day proved to be a revelation for all. Alair was indeed amazed at everything that he saw and the others saw their surroundings in a new light. They enjoyed themselves and returned to the farm laden with packages, not all of them for Amey. The Magician's car was still there.

Amey spent her afternoon putting her new things together for her trip back to school on the early morning train. Lirin leaned back on her bed while Amey packed her bag keeping their conversation light and entertaining. He was happy to see the shadows gone from Amey's eyes.

The evening passed quietly. Amey showed her father more pictures and other treasures that she had collected over the years. She told him stories and listened as he talked about his youth. Rose and Angeline added their reminiscences. There was a strong bond developing between Alair and her father. Angeline and Rose exchanged a smile as they watched the two identical heads looking at the various things that were being shared.

They retired early and were up with the sun the next morning. They were a cheerful group that piled into the car for the trip to the train station. They stood together on the platform waiting for the train and chatted easily. When it pulled into the station, Alair turned to Amey and put his arms around her.

"Take good care of yourself and we will see you in June. I want you to have this."

He pulled a chain from around his neck and slipped it over her head. Suspended from it was a gold cross.

"This was my mother's. She wore it all the time. It was given to me when your mother and I married. I was to give it to your mother but things happened so fast after my parents' deaths that I forgot about it. Now that I have a daughter, I want you to have it. Your Mother agrees."

Amey looked down at the cross running her finger over the delicate carving. She looked up at her father with tears in her eyes.

"Thank you. I will treasure this as another link to my family."

Rose smiled and kissed Amey on the cheek. She hugged her tightly as if she didn't want to let her go.

"We are looking forward to the summer. I can't wait until we can spend some quiet time together. Your father and I will do all we can to find the hermit for you. Take care, Amey. Be safe. I love you so much!"

Angeline and then Jasper said their goodbyes in turn. Lirin waited until Amey was about to board the train and held out his hand.

"When do you get out of school?"

"Mid-June. We have our exams the second week and then we can go right after that."

"Then I will see you in June. Be safe."

Amey smiled and started to turn away. At the last minute, she swung around and caught Lirin by surprise by hugging him and kissing him on the cheek.

"See you in June."

She quickly climbed the stairs and went to her seat, choosing one on the side where she could see her family. They stood together smiling at her. When the train started to move, they followed along waving to her. Lirin smiled and mouthed the words, "Till June."

Amey watched and waved until the train pulled out of the station. She sat down and her hand went to the cross her father gave her. She smiled and leaned back in her seat. She thought about the last moments on the platform and looked forward to a bright future.

No one noticed the figure lurking in the shadows of the station.

The End

Heartfelt thanks to the people who encouraged me by reading the rough drafts:
To the Voices in Bloom group (Laurie, Tammy, Harriet, Kathy T., Dawna)
Dorothy, Ashley, Marci, Ev, Kathy and Carsten.

Don't miss out!

Visit the website below and you can sign up to receive emails whenever Kathleen L. Moore publishes a new book. There's no charge and no obligation.

https://books2read.com/r/B-A-KCOM-AREDC

BOOKS 2 READ

Connecting independent readers to independent writers.

About the Author

I am a mother of 3 and grandmother of 6 and live in the remote Bella Coola Valley on the Central Coast of British Columbia, Canada. I grew up in Ontario and our family moved here in 1974. We have been self-employed since 1995 running a small greenhouse business for 26 years.

I have written stories and poetry all my life. In 1969, I won the Birks Award for English. I am a visual artist in pen and ink and watercolour and I have shown my work in several exhibitions and created the cover for my book 'The Jewelled Kingdom'. My approach to writing is also very visual. I am also part of a Voices in Bloom group who meet monthly on Zoom.

This is my first book although I have written prose and poetry for many years from childhood with some of my poetry being used for various celebrations.

CPSIA information can be obtained
at www.ICGtesting.com
Printed in the USA
BVHW051441060323
659783BV00006B/66

9 798215 858028